A wedding dilemma:

What should a sexy, successful bachelor do
if he's too busy making millions to find a wife?
Or if he finds the perfect woman, and just *has* to
strike a bridal bargain...?

The perfect proposal:

The solution? For better, for worse, these grooms
in a hurry have decided to sign, seal and deliver
the ultimate marriage contract....

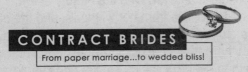

CONTRACT BRIDES
From paper marriage...to wedded bliss!

Look out for our next CONTRACT BRIDES story,
coming soon in Harlequin Romance®!

Barbara McMahon was born and raised in the South, but settled in California after spending a year flying around the world for an international airline. After settling down to raise a family and work for a computer firm, she began writing when her children started school. Now, feeling fortunate in being able to realize a long-held dream of quitting her "day job" and writing full-time, she and her husband have moved to the Sierra Nevada of California, where she finds her desire to write is stronger than ever. With the beauty of the mountains visible from her windows, and the pace of life slower than the hectic San Francisco Bay area where they previously resided, she finds more time than ever to think up stories and characters and share them with others through writing. Barbara loves to hear from readers. You can reach her at P.O. Box 977, Pioneer, CA 95666-0977, U.S.A. Readers can also contact Barbara at her Web site: www.barbaramcmahon.com

Look out for Barbara's next book
His Convenient Fiancée
On sale November 2004 in Harlequin Romance®!

MARRIAGE IN NAME ONLY

Barbara McMahon

CONTRACT BRIDES

From paper marriage...to wedded bliss!

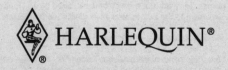

HARLEQUIN®

TORONTO • NEW YORK • LONDON
AMSTERDAM • PARIS • SYDNEY • HAMBURG
STOCKHOLM • ATHENS • TOKYO • MILAN • MADRID
PRAGUE • WARSAW • BUDAPEST • AUCKLAND

To Charles Nash, for teaching me I can do anything I want, and for always being there for me. I love you, Daddy!

ISBN 0-373-18159-0

MARRIAGE IN NAME ONLY

First North American Publication 2004.

Copyright © 2004 by Barbara McMahon.

www.eHarlequin.com

Printed in U.S.A.

CHAPTER ONE

"I HATE winter," Jenny said softly to herself, scowling at the leaden skies visible through the tall windows surrounding the large open lobby of Rocky Point Inn. Absently she rubbed her aching leg. Better than Pete Dowling on the Six O'clock News Team for predicting the weather, she thought wryly. Of course it didn't take a rocket scientist to know Maine in winter was cold, with snow either falling or on the way.

Despite being dressed in wool slacks, a thick cable-knit sweater and warm socks and shoes, she felt chilled. The roaring fire across the room, flanked by sofas and easy chairs, gave an illusion of warmth. Maybe if she were closer, without the width of the room and barrier of the reception counter between her and the hearth, she would feel more of the heat.

The lobby was deserted. She didn't normally work the registration desk, but she was still shorthanded, and when Libby had asked for time off to go to Portland for a special afternoon with her granddaughter, Jenny had said yes. It was a slow week. And a few hours on the front desk was easy duty.

She glanced at the clock. It wasn't even four, but the darkening skies would bring night earlier than usual. She'd have to call Angie soon. That child would skate until dark-thirty if she were allowed.

For a moment Jenny's heart softened. If it gave the little girl joy, she'd let her skate as long as she could in good consciousness. She knew all too well the pain of losing her parents. At least she'd been nineteen when her father died, not eight like Angie. And to lose both parents at once was devastating. If the little girl could forgot the tragedy briefly when she skated, Jenny was all for letting her skate as long as there was daylight.

She rubbed her hip, and shifted on the high stool behind the counter. She couldn't get comfortable. Maybe she should walk around and see if that would ease the discomfort. It never did, but she tried a variety of things when the ache became intolerable. A hot bath sometimes helped, but she couldn't leave the desk.

One of the heavy double doors thrust open. Jenny looked up and stared. She wasn't expecting anyone—certainly not a man like this! He was dressed totally in black, from scuffed motorcycle boots, up legs encased in black cords, to a broad chest covered by a black shirt and black leather jacket. The jacket was open, swinging as he headed directly toward the desk. He carried a beat-up duffel bag over his shoulder and a black leather laptop case in one hand.

He wasn't from around here, Jenny thought, struck by his rugged good looks. Not with that tan. He walked across the lobby as if he owned the place, bold and confident. Further speculation ended when he stopped right in front of her. His dark eyes stared right back at her. His windswept black hair attested to the storm front moving in.

For a moment time hung suspended. He was tall, more than six feet, Jenny guessed. And with a watchfulness about him that attested to the fact he didn't take things on face value. She'd never seen him before, she would have remembered!

"May I help you?" she asked.

"Got a room?" His teeth were white against the dark tan when he smiled. His skin crinkled a bit at the corner of his eyes, a hint of sadness hidden in their depths. He went through the motions, but she had a feeling he was keeping his emotions firmly in check. Who was he and what was he doing in Rocky Point, Maine? He was definitely not her usual type of guest.

She nodded. They had several unoccupied bedrooms this week. Vacant even through the weekend, though business would pick up after that. The February Festival started soon.

"I'll take it," he said, dumping the duffel bag and carefully placing the laptop case on the floor. He reached for his wallet.

"How long will you be staying?" Jenny took one of the registration cards and slid it toward him. Electricity seemed to shimmer in the air. She forgot about being cold, and her aching leg. Her curiosity was piqued for the first time in ages.

"As short a time as possible." He took the pen and began to fill out the card.

He was too early for the college's February Festival. That wouldn't start for another week and a half. Thankfully for her bottom line, she was booked solid for that week, and the two weekends flanking the annual event.

But this week, the Inn was almost empty. Only two older couples, alumni of Blackstone College, were staying, having come to Rocky Point for a walk down memory lane. The weather didn't seem to bother them any more than it appeared to bother this man. She wished she was as lucky to not feel the chill in the air all the time.

"Isn't it cold out?" she asked to make conversation. His leather jacket didn't seem warm enough for the cold spell they were having. Her curiosity notched up. Was he a visiting professor at the college? He didn't seem the type, but she knew teachers came in all kinds of packages these days. What would he teach—motorcycle 101?

"Colder than a wi—never mind. It's cold. Made worse because I just got off a diving trip to Tahiti and no sooner landed in L.A. than I had to catch a flight here— in February of all times. I don't mind Snowbird or Alta in winter, but the Maine coast is the last place I wanted to come in this time of year. Or any time, actually!"

She blinked at the picture he painted.

Diving in Tahiti. Skiing in the Rockies. She studied him as he completed the registration card. His shirt covered a strongly masculine body in excellent condition. Wide shoulders, narrow hips, not an ounce of superfluous fat anywhere she could see. He was probably naturally athletic, enjoying sports of all kinds. He moved with ease, comfortable in his own body, and its capabilities. It went with the arrogance he couldn't conceal. Hot sex in black jeans.

Jenny looked away, shocked at her thoughts. She hadn't had a reaction like that in a long time. Cool your jets, girl, she admonished herself. He's not for you.

Envy and a wistful regret washed through her. He represented everything she had lost, and would never again enjoy. She had grown up around the type, brash and arrogant and gorgeous—and knew it. Woman everywhere probably flocked around him.

Not her. Not that he'd ever glance her way. Or that she wanted him to.

He gave her a cocky grin and shoved the card to her. It was second nature to him, she could tell.

"Any place to eat around here?" he asked.

Even his voice sounded different, more of a drawl than the clipped New England tones she was used to. Dark and slightly husky. She wondered what it would sound like if he was sweet-talking some willing woman.

''The Inn's restaurant will be opened at six. We serve dinner until eight.'' Her own voice sounded prissy, she couldn't help it—instinctive reaction to the pull of attraction that surprised her. He was just a guest, for heaven's sake, not someone to fantasize about.

''What if I want something later?''

''There is a vending machine at the end of the second floor with assorted snacks. Otherwise, I'm afraid you'd have to go into town.''

''The center of which looks to be two blocks over, and one block long''

''We may not be as big as Los Angeles, but we have all you could need,'' Jenny snapped. If he didn't like the town, why come? She was overreacting, she knew that. But he rubbed her the wrong way. Was it his manner, or just the memories of all she could no longer do?

She leaned back and snagged a key for room seven. It was a corner room, and as far from the stairs as possible. It was petty, with other rooms vacant, but she didn't care. She didn't like the stranger. Didn't like what he represented. He reminded her of Karl. Let him walk the extra distance.

"And how late are the places in town open?"

"The Dairy Haven on the highway is open until eleven. They serve burgers, fries and ice cream. The Rose In Bloom Café is open until nine, eleven on weekends."

He shook his head, and lifted the laptop. "I can see dinner here sounds like the best bet." Taking the key he started toward the stairs. Jenny watched him stop and turn back.

"Know where Jennifer Gordon is?"

Foreboding filled her. Who was he? Why did he want to know where she was?

"Why?"

"I'm Connor Wolfe, here to get my niece. She's watching her."

"You're Angie's uncle?" It had been almost three months since a raging house fire had killed both Cathy and Harrison Benson, Angie's parents. The authorities had been trying for weeks to locate any next of kin, finally coming up with Cathy's only brother. With the fire consuming every scrap of information about Cathy's family, it had been a long slow process. Angie hadn't known anything about her uncle beyond his first name.

Everyone had known Harrison forever, he'd been born and raised right in Rocky Point. But he had no kin living, so Cathy's brother was the only hope.

Fortunately for Angie, Rocky Point was basically a small town, despite the college which swelled its population each school term. Sheriff Tucker had allowed Angie to stay with Jenny until her uncle could be located and notified. The arrangement saved worrying the bureaucrats at Children's Services in Portland, and allowed Angie to stay in a place she knew and was comfortable. Cathy had worked for Jenny. The two of them had been fast friends for years. Angie had come to the Inn after school every day until it was time for them to return home. She knew Jenny well. And Jenny was happy to care for her friend's daughter—until her next of kin arrived.

''I didn't know Angie's uncle had been located,'' Jenny said slowly, looking at the registration card. It had been so long, she'd wondered if they would ever find him.

"And you should know that because?" he asked.

"Because I'm Jenny Gordon. Angie's been staying with me. Isaac didn't tell me you were coming."

"Isaac being?"

"The sheriff."

"Right, I met him. I stopped there when I arrived. He recommended this place, as a matter of fact. Makes sense now. I can't help if he told you or not. I arrived back in L.A. yesterday, got this note about Cathy. I caught a red-eye to Boston last night and here I am. This isn't the easiest place in the world to get to."

"He didn't mention it to me." Why hadn't he? He'd know Jenny would want to know. If for no other reason than to prepare Angie.

Connor shrugged. "Not my problem. Is my niece here?"

"She's outside playing. She'll be in soon. I can call her now if you like." Jenny wondered how Angie would take to this stranger. He was certainly different from her bluff, happy-go-lucky father.

He hesitated a moment, then shook his head. "Let her play. Time enough to meet her later. I'm going up to drop this stuff."

He turned and started to climb the stairs.

"I'm sorry about your sister," Jenny called. "Cathy was one of my best friends. I miss her like crazy."

He glanced back down toward the desk, his face in shadow. "I didn't see her much in recent years, but I never thought she'd die so young."

Jenny watched until he was out of sight, her dislike taking a new twist. He hadn't asked a thing about Angie, not how was she doing, not how she was taking her parents' death. He evidenced no impatience to even see her. Didn't he realize she was a little girl who had just suffered a traumatic loss? Jenny thought he should have shown more interest.

From the conversations Jenny had had with Cathy over the years, and the recent lopsided conversations with Angie, she knew the family ties had not been close. Connor Wolfe had never come to see Cathy in the ten years she lived in Rocky Point. Nor had she, to Jenny's knowledge, gone to visit her brother.

To Angie, uncle or not, he was a total stranger.

The front door opened again. Angie bounded in, her cheeks rosy from the cold, her light brown eyes sparkling with delight, lashes shimmering with snowflakes. Ice skates hung over her shoulder, one in front, one in back, banging against her as she almost flew across the lobby and around the back of the counter.

"It was great, Jenny. I almost did a spin. But then my blade caught on something and I fell on my butt. Andy laughed, but Cilla said practice makes perfect, so I tried again. But then it began to snow which mucked up the ice. I'm hungry, what can I have to eat?"

Jenny smiled at Angie's exuberance. She could remember feeling the same way so long ago.

"Dry your blades and put your skates up. You can go ask Mrs. Thompson for a light snack, but don't spoil your appetite. We'll be eating dinner in a couple of hours. Then homework!"

"I only have spelling and math," Angie shouted as she raced across the lobby and clattered up the stairs.

Jenny knew she should have said something to Angie about her uncle's arrival. But the middle of a public lobby where privacy couldn't be guaranteed wasn't the place. She'd explain at dinner, and hope the two of them didn't meet before Jenny had a chance to warn Angie.

Warn her? About what? Her uncle had come to take her home to live with him. It appeared he lived in Los Angeles, far from anything Angie had known in her short life. Jenny wondered if the man would consider staying in Rocky Point for a while until Angie got used to the changes. Staying would enable her to get to know him better while she was still surrounded by friends and familiar settings.

But there was not a chance of him staying, she was sure, from his cryptic comment when signing in. She wanted to sweep Angie away and protect her from any future hurts. She had a feeling it would be a big job.

Connor entered the Inn's dining room shortly after six. It was earlier than he normally ate, but with the time changes and nonstop traveling for two days, he wasn't sure where he should be in the meal schedule. He was hungry, he would eat.

There were about eighteen tables in the large room, only one of which was occupied. Two couples chatted together, oblivious to anything or anyone else.

He nodded when a waitress came from the kitchen, carrying salads.

"Have a seat anywhere, I'll be right with you," she called. From the looks of her, she was one of the students from Blackstone College. Connor remembered bits and pieces of the few, infrequent letters Cathy had sent. She'd taken a couple of courses at the college when she'd first moved to Rocky Point. Before Angie had been born. Maybe he'd check out the college before he left. He'd already seen most of the town. He couldn't imagine his sister living here. He wished he'd taken the time to make at least one visit while she'd been alive.

Connor chose a table near the window, unable to see anything in the stygian darkness except the swirling snow illuminated by the light from the window. The predicted storm had arrived.

He hoped it wouldn't hold up things. He wanted to leave early in the morning. With the right connections, he and Angie could be back in L.A. by dinner tomorrow. He had his secretary looking into things. How long could it take to pack up a little girl's possessions—especially when everything she owned prior to three months ago burned in the house fire?

Connor clenched his jaw and gazed blankly from the window. He and Cathy had not been close. They hadn't even seen each other in more than a decade. But she had been his younger sister and the only relative he cared to acknowledge. She died too young.

Had she known the outcome, would she still have moved to Rocky Point and lived the life of a fisherman's wife?

He remembered their last fight. He'd been incredulous that she wanted to move to the back of beyond. She complained she was tired of life in impersonal Los Angeles. Cathy wanted family, roots and a place to grow old around long-time friends. She had wanted so much more than they'd had growing up. Connor hoped she'd found it.

"Mr. Wolfe?" The young waitress stood by his table, offering a menu. "Jenny said she'll be in the office if you wish to speak with her after your dinner. It's the door right by the reception desk with a sign saying Office."

He nodded. She waited to one side while he reviewed the selections. When he gave her his choices, she headed for the kitchen.

The meal was excellent, though Connor didn't notice. He was surprised Jennifer Gordon hadn't brought his niece to meet him. Surely the child couldn't still be playing outside. Maybe that was the reason for the meeting in the office—a formal introduction. Did she know he had never seen his niece? Of course she would, if nothing else the child would have told her.

Neither he nor Cathy had been great in the letter writing arena. A Christmas card from her, occasionally a birthday card if she remembered. A handful of infrequent letters. He had his secretary keep track of the holidays and birthdays, sending cards, enclosing a check when his circumstances had improved. But he couldn't remember a single thing he'd learned from Cathy about her daughter, or her life in Rocky Point, beyond she was happy and loved her husband. Her letters had tapered off over the last few years.

He hadn't a clue what to do with an eight-year-old, boy or girl. He'd never married and didn't associate with married couples. He was footloose and fancy free as the saying went—and determined to remain that way.

His secretary would handle Angie. He just had to get back to L.A.

Refusing dessert, he rose when he'd finished and headed for Jennifer Gordon's office. Might as well get the ball rolling.

There was another young college student behind the registration desk this evening, a young man in a white shirt and tie. Training for hotel management, Connor suspected from the determined look on his face. Maybe he'd head up a major chain one day. He nodded to the younger man and knocked on the half opened door marked Office.

"Come in." The same soft voice from that afternoon.

Connor stepped inside and shut the door behind him. She sat behind a large desk and looked up when he entered. Gesturing to one of the two chair pushed against the wall, she waited until he pulled one closer to the desk and sat, resting one ankle on his knee.

Her dark hair was pulled back and tied at the nape of her neck. Her large blue eyes watched him warily. For a moment he felt a sense of recognition. But he'd never been here before. Could their paths have crossed elsewhere?

Her bulky white cable sweater enveloped her, but he could see she was slender, with curves in the right places. He wondered at her serious demeanor. She hadn't even smiled when he arrived—before she knew who he was. Did that have a bearing on anything?

"I checked with Isaac and then spoke with Angie," she began without further ado. "You are apparently her uncle. Isaac said he left a message yesterday after confirming the relationship. Apparently the message got misplaced. I'm sorry I wasn't expecting you. It's been so long." She took a breath. "Anyway, welcome."

"No harm done. Angie knows?"

Jenny nodded. "I told her over dinner. She is—" she faltered for a moment, as if looking for the correct word, "interested in meeting you. I thought you two might do better if I were present, since Angie has known me all her life. But I can leave you alone, if you'd rather."

"I can tell by your tone, you don't think that's the best plan." Hell, he was starting to feel nervous. About an eight-year-old girl? He was never nervous. Multimillion dollar deals, a piece of cake. Deep-sea diving, exciting. Daring rock climbing exploits, exhilarating. He was not nervous about meeting his niece!

"You are a total stranger to her, and she has just lost both her parents. It would be hard for anyone, don't you think?" Jenny asked.

The soul of reason. Since Connor hadn't been looking forward to this meeting, he could imagine a little kid would have similar apprehensions.

"Send for her. You can make the introductions. We'll see how it goes from there."

Jenny reached for the phone and dialed upstairs. Speaking quickly, she hung up. Then, she waited, her eyes on the door—almost as if she were trying to ignore him. He had no similar compunctions. He stared, feeling a sense of elation when color flooded her cheeks. She wasn't as impervious as she'd like to pretend.

"I'll be taking her off your hands tomorrow," he said.

She inclined her head once. "She's been no trouble. I was glad to have her here. Cathy worked for me, you know, as well as being my friend. I'll always miss her. As I'm sure Angie will. Do you want to extend your visit or are you making other arrangements? Angie has been staying in my private apartment, which she can continue to do if you like. Or I can make another room available for her if you prefer.''

''We'll be leaving for L.A. in the morning.''

''What?'' That caused her to swing around to stare at him in horror. ''You can't do that!''

''Why not?''

There was a soft knock on the door. Before Jenny could call out, Angie opened it and stuck her head in. ''I'm here.''

''Come in, sweetie, and close the door behind you,'' Jenny said.

Connor was struck first by how small the child was. Then how hesitant. She didn't display any of the bold, sassy confidence he remembered in his sister. Angie walked over behind the desk and leaned against Jenny, studying him warily.

''Angie, this is your uncle, Connor Wolfe, your mama's brother. Mr. Wolfe, this is Angie Benton.''

''Call me Connor,'' he murmured, his eyes never leaving Angie's. ''Hello, Angie.''

''Hello.'' She pressed closer to Jenny. ''You don't look like my mama.''

''No, we didn't look much alike. I remember when she was your age, though. She loved to swim. Do you like to swim?''

''In summer.''

''Where I live you can swim all year along.''

''Where's that?''

''In Southern California. It's warm there all year long.''

She darted a scared glance at Jenny. ''I don't have to go to California, do I?''

''Honey, your uncle just got here. We have lots to discuss. Nothing has been decided yet. You'll be the first to know when it is. You and your uncle need to get to know one another. Maybe you can take him up and show him your room, and your homework and things. Tomorrow when you get home from school, you can introduce him to Andy and Cilla.''

''Tomorrow we'll be airborne—''

''*Not. Now!*'' Jenny interrupted, glaring at him.

Connor was taken aback. It had been years since anyone had flat out shut him up. He hadn't built his company into a multimillion dollar concern by taking that from anyone. But the glare in her eyes didn't fade. The little innkeeper began to irritate him. Just who did she think she was?

"We have nothing to discuss, Ms. Gordon. We'll fly home in the morning. My secretary is already looking into boarding schools. She'll be set before you know it."

"Boarding school?" Jenny said, horrified.

"What's a boarding school?" Angie asked looking puzzled.

"It's nothing you have to worry about just yet," Jenny said, eyes flashing at Connor. "Why don't you go ask Mrs. Thompson for some of her nice brownies. You can bring a plate of them back here for all of us to share. Okay?"

"Okay, I love brownies." Angie took off at a run, without a glance at her uncle. Once the door closed behind her, Jenny rounded on him.

"Mr. Wolfe, you cannot take this child off tomorrow and then shunt her into some *boarding school!* She has just lost both parents. Not to mention every material thing she ever owned. The only stable things she has left are her friends, her routine and her school. You want to yank that all away and stuff her in some impersonal boarding school? Impossible. I won't let you!''

''And how do you plan to stop me, Ms. Gordon. I'm her next of kin. What I says goes. And I say we leave for L.A. in the morning.'' The sooner things got settled, the better. It had been three months since the accident, but he'd only learned of it yesterday. It still hit him hard. Not that he planned to let Jenny Gordon know. It was none of her damned business the regrets he faced.

She rose and leaned against the desk, anger causing her to blush. Connor swore sparks were shooting from her eyes.

''No one can be that cruel to a little girl. She needs to be around people she knows, trusts, loves. You are a stranger to her. At least consider staying for a little while, until she gets to know you. Maybe you'll feel differently, as well. She doesn't deserve a boarding school. She's only eight. She needs a home, family, people she can relate to and count on.''

''And I have a company to run in L.A. I don't live in the wilds of Maine. I don't have a lot of time to stay here and get to know her. We have the rest of our lives to get to know each other. And a home sounds fine, but I can't take care of a kid. I don't know the first thing about children.'' Connor rose and leaned against the opposite side of the desk until his nose was only inches from hers. "I don't have a lot of choices here. I live in a high-rise, adult apartment complex, no place for kids. There's no one home to take care of her during the day, even if it allowed children. Boarding school is the only alternative. Unless you want me to leave her with you."

Jenny felt her heart catch. She would love to have Angie live with her. But it wouldn't work. Slowly the anger faded and anguished regret took its place.

She sank down in her chair, her gaze going unseeing to the blotter in the center of the desk.

"No, she can't stay with me," she said softly.

"Then another family in town?"

"I don't know. Maybe." She looked up hopefully. "Would you at least explore that possibility? It beats a boarding school."

She could tell he was weighing the options. Was he giving any weight to Angie's emotional well being? Or was she just some inconvenience to be shunted off and forgotten?

''Very well, I'll stay a couple of days. But I expect you to help. Find a family who might be willing to take her on.''

''I'd be glad to.'' A reprieve. Jenny felt as if a weight had been lifted. Nothing had been decided and she wasn't at all certain any family in town would be able to take Angie. No one had come forward since the fire. And it was a huge responsibility, raising a child. But she could try.

Of course, the entire town knew Angie was staying with Jenny. But that would never work long term. Jenny couldn't be depended upon, everyone knew that. A woman who let down her own father, her partner, the entire town—how could she become responsible for raising a child?

CHAPTER TWO

CONNOR rose early, despite the constant travel and half a dozen time zones he'd been in the last few days. He showered, shaved and dressed before dawn even showed on the horizon. Gazing out at the darkness, he stepped near the window, seeing the snow piles beneath the lights in the parking area, and on the streets. Standing close to the window, he could feel the cool air from the panes. Three days ago he'd been in his own cottage on a sugar white sand beach in Tahiti. No panes in those windows, just shutters to close in the case of tropical storms. Otherwise the balmy scented air flowed through the rooms like a caress.

Now he was in the frigid winter of Maine. Life played funny tricks sometimes.

He checked his watch. Still the middle of the night in L.A. He'd have to give Stephanie a chance to get to work before calling her to let her know he would be a day or two later in returning. He'd already been gone for several weeks, she always held the fort. She could continue to do so another couple of days. At least now, she could reach him by phone.

Stephanie had been with him since the startup. She'd been a struggling single mom in those days, grateful for a job and willing to work as long hours as he had. Now she was married to a physician and both her children were in college. She no longer worked the same long hours. But she was outstanding at what she did, and he relied on her heavily.

Good fortune smiled on them both. Until now.

He turned away. If only it had continued to smile on Cathy. She had been too young to die.

He hoped Jenny Gordon would find some prospective families who might take Angie. He'd pay support, that wasn't difficult. Arranging to have her in his life was proving the problem. He had never expected to have a child. Marriage and commitment weren't something he ever thought about. He'd seen what family ties could do with his own parents. Watching various friends' divorces over the years had strengthened his resolve. The single life was for him, meeting new experiences unencumbered, exploring new places with no one to complain he didn't give them enough attention. Avoiding the emotional quagmire that relationships seemed to engender was the only way to go.

He suspected Jenny Gordon was tradition bound, probably eighth generation Rocky Pointer or some such thing. A Mayflower descendant for all he knew.

Odd that she seemed to like Angie so much and yet wouldn't consider taking her on full time. She'd had her for three months. Maybe she was looking for some compensation. He hadn't mentioned money last night. It usually opened a lot of doors, he thought cynically. With Angie already settled here, it would be the easiest solution.

What time did that dining room open for breakfast, wasn't it seven? He'd go down to see. Nothing else to do until the West Coast woke up.

Entering the dining room a few minutes later, Connor saw Jenny sitting at the same small table he'd used last night. She was halfway through a plate of eggs and sausage. She sipped a cup of coffee. Beyond her, dawn was just showing through the window.

He crossed over and placed his hand on the back of the second chair. "May I?"

She looked startled to see him. Glancing around as if letting him know every other table in the place was available, she shrugged. "I guess so."

"Good morning to you, too," he said, sitting down and studying her. "Are you the manager here?"

"I own the Inn."

"So it's hard to escalate a complaint when you don't make a guest feel welcomed."

"You are hardly a guest," Jenny replied, her gaze locking with his.

Connor knew he made her angry, he just wasn't sure why. He'd sensed it yesterday before she'd known who he was.

"What else would I be?"

Her gaze became speculative. "Almost family?"

"By way of my niece?"

She nodded.

An older woman peeped out from the kitchen. "I thought I heard voices. What can I get you?" she asked Connor, stepping into the dining room.

"Huevos Rancheros, and a pot of black coffee."

"Coming right up!"

"Is that the same cook who made dinner last night?" he asked.

"Yes. She works a split shift, breakfast and dinners. The Inn doesn't serve lunch. Mrs. Thompson's wonderful. Did you enjoy dinner?"

"It was delicious. You're lucky to get someone so talented here."

"In the back of beyond, do you mean?" Jenny asked, almost smiling. Did everyone in L.A. think it was the center of the universe?

And why not, most folks in Rocky Point thought their hometown was the center!

"She obviously wants to live here. With her talent, she could find a position anywhere. How about you? Born and raised here?" Connor asked.

"Yes."

"Confirms a theory."

"What theory," she asked.

"That you were born and bred here, never wanted to leave. There are two kinds of folks. Those like you and those like me," he said.

"And you're the rolling stone?"

"Get to see a lot of the world that way. Never could see the appeal of staying in one spot for endless years."

"There certainly is an appeal. You get to know your neighbors, know what to expect in life. Find a niche and you're happy to be part of the community. But I haven't always lived here. I've seen my share of the world," she said. Then frowned. That portion of her life was not something she spoke of these days. Why had she felt compelled to mention it to Connor Wolfe? Something about him rubbed her the wrong way. It did not invite confidences, but she wanted to show him she wasn't the bucolic woman, content to rusticate in some backwater town in Maine.

"So you've seen the world and came back here? Boring. Though that was what Cathy was searching for. A quiet place to belong."

"She found it here," Jenny said, refusing to rise to the bait he dangled by insulting her town. Her best plan would be deal with him as efficiently as possible, try to get him to do the best for Angie, and then say goodbye.

"Did she?" He went still, the intensity of his gaze almost painful to see.

"She was happy here, if that's what you want to know. She relished small town life. Trust me, we had lots of long philosophical discussions revolving around Rocky Point. She adored Harrison and Angie, enjoyed being part of a community that has been around since before the Revolution. Liked tradition, customs and all the routine that normal living brings. She was a lot better at it than I am."

"Ever want to leave?" he asked.

"I had my shot at the gold, saw some sights I'd never thought to see. Now I'm content to stay here and operate my Inn." Jenny had quelled the longings, had denied her dreams. She would likely remain in Rocky Point until she died. She could have had a worse fate.

"Don't you long to travel?"

"Some things are not meant to be. And some things are. Here's Sally with your Huevos Rancheros."

"Sort of a fatalistic point of view."

"I don't wish to discuss philosophy with you, Mr. Wolfe. I want to discuss Angie before she joins us."

"She'll be down for breakfast?"

"Soon. She has to leave for school at

eight-fifteen. Do you want to meet her teacher today?"

"Why?"

"Aren't you at all interested in this child? She's your sister's daughter. You're all she's got."

He took a bite of eggs, chewed slowly, his gaze never leaving hers. He could correct that assumption, but didn't. No need for anyone in town to know about his father. God, what a mess that would be if the old man learned of Angie's situation. When he swallowed, he answered frankly, "I don't know much about children. You're saying I should meet her teacher? I thought I was scheduled to meet her friends after school."

"That, too. When you were growing up, didn't your parents take an interest in school?"

"Your small town roots are showing, Jenny Gordon. First of all, I didn't have parents when I was growing up. I had my old man. Solo. My mother split about the time I turned five and Cathy was a baby. She took the girl, he kept the boy. Neither one of them should have had kids." He hadn't had any contact with his father in years. It would suit him to keep it that way forever. His mother hadn't been much better.

"Occasionally my father would remember he had a kid he was responsible for. I'd get a bunch of new clothes, a toy or two, and then it was on my own again until the next time he remembered," he finished.

Jenny opened her mouth as if to say something and promptly closed it. If she didn't like the bleak picture he painted, tough. Maybe it was time she knew the facts of life. Not everyone had a fairy-tale childhood.

Connor was on a roll. This prissy woman from the centuries-old family thought she knew the answers. He continued to enlighten her.

"My mother visited once or twice a year and brought Cathy. We had nothing in common but a blood tie."

"I knew some of that," she said softly a hint of sympathy in her tone. "Cathy spoke of her mother, and how hard it had been growing up in L.A. How much more she wanted for Angie."

Connor frowned. He was the last man to need anyone's sympathy. He'd come from nothing, but made a good life for himself. He could buy and sell Jennifer Gordon's little Inn, and not notice the dent in his finances. If Cathy had stayed in L.A., she could have had a share in the business. And she'd probably be alive today.

"Hi Jenny," Angie called from the doorway, her face bright with a smile. She dumped her backpack in a chair near the door and walked to the table, her gaze warily on Connor. When she drew near Jenny, she smiled shyly at her uncle.

"Good morning," she said.

"How are you today?" he asked, glad for the interruption. What had he been thinking spilling his guts to Jenny Gordon? He never told anyone about his past. Now, after less than twenty-four hours, he'd told her more than he even liked remembering.

He looked at the two of them facing him. Both had identical wary expressions that were starting to drive him crazy.

"We're not going anywhere today," he told Angie. The relief was almost palatable.

"After school, want to come watch me skate?" she asked.

"And meet your friends," he said, with a glance at Jenny. Her smile startled him. And unsettled him. For the first time he looked at her as a woman. An elegant one with high cheekbones and fine skin. Again he had the feeling he knew her. He'd seen her somewhere before. Where? If she knew him, why not mention it?

"Run and tell Mrs. Thompson you're ready for breakfast. It snowed a lot last night and you'll want to stay warm walking to school."

"I can give her a ride," Connor said. Maybe kids were hardier in Maine, but no sense in her having to plough through the drifts going to school when he had the rental SUV.

"Will your car handle the snow? I don't know if all the roads are clear yet."

"I rented a four wheel drive. You don't normally take her? There's no bus?"

"She usually walks. The buses are for the kids in outlying areas. The school isn't far."

"Mrs. Thompson is bringing me oatmeal. With brown sugar," Angie said, bursting out from the kitchen and rushing to her backpack. She withdrew a paper and ran to the table and thrust it out to Jenny.

"Can you say my spelling words?" She looked at Connor. "You're sitting in my place." Before he could respond, she turned and pulled a chair from a neighboring table and sat on the side.

He looked at Jenny. "You two usually eat breakfast together?"

"Yes. We eat all our meals together, except when Angie is in school."

"Do you want me to leave?"

Jenny shook her head. "Finish your breakfast. I'm through and when Mrs. Thompson brings the oatmeal, she can clear my place, giving Angie plenty of room." She looked at the page and then spoke a word.

Angie spelled it perfectly. Jenny said another.

Connor felt as if he were floating above them in the room, seeing all three from a distance, sitting cozily at a breakfast table. Just like countless families across the country were probably doing at this same moment. Jenny grilling Angie on spelling words, the three sharing a meal, normal daily routines.

He felt uncomfortable. He'd never been part of a meal like this, not when he was a kid and certainly not since he'd grown up.

It looked right, with Jenny and Angie working together. In fact, unless he missed his guess, Jenny and Angie had a special bond between them. So what was the problem with Jenny taking Angie instead of trying to foist her off on some other family in town?

Complications with a boyfriend who didn't want children?

He frowned. It was none of his business if that were the case. He took another look at Jenny. The thick sweater she wore couldn't totally conceal the curves and valley of her figure. Her face was animated when dealing with Angie, beautiful with faint pink color in her cheeks and a sparkle in her eyes. He wondered how her hair felt. Its glossy black sheen caught the lights from the chandeliers and gleamed. He bet it would be silky soft. It was so smooth pulled against her head, but would it flow like silk when released from confinement?

A flare of interest and awareness flashed. His gaze shifted to her mouth, most of the lipstick was gone. Still her lips looked soft and pink, the lower lip slightly fuller than the upper.

She glanced at him, her expression puzzled. Caught staring like a randy teenager, he frowned and looked away, finishing his meal. He waited for a break in the spelling quiz and rose.

"I'll give you a ride to school, Angie, if you can direct me," he said doing his best to put any carnal thoughts of Jenny Gordon firmly from his mind. He was here for his niece, not to fantasize about some woman he'd just met. One, moreover he knew was probably into commitment, marriage and happy ever after, not a one-night stand.

The little girl looked at Jenny for approval. She nodded. "It's okay if you want him to. Uncle Connor wants to see your school, maybe meet your teacher."

"Okay. I'll be ready in just a minute. I need to finish my oatmeal."

Uncle Connor. It sounded odd to hear someone speak so calmly of his new role. "Take your time, I'll get my jacket and wait for you in the lobby," he said beating a hasty retreat.

He wasn't running away, just withdrawing to better strategize. The last thing he needed was an attraction to his niece's— what? What was Jenny to Angie? Or for that matter, what was she to him? Someone he'd just met. So what if she was pretty. He'd just returned from Tahiti, where he'd seen plenty of beautiful women.

Connor strode from the room, his libido firmly in check. He'd get to know Angie, determine what would be best for her, and leave. With or without his niece remained to be seen. Either way, Miss Rocky Point would remain safely in her Inn where she apparently preferred to be.

"Ready, Uncle Connor," Angie greeted him when he came back down a few minutes later. If he were going to stay for any length of time, a warmer jacket would be required. He frowned, not liking that thought. He hoped to clear everything up in a day or two and head back to Los Angeles.

"Let's go, kid." He wasn't sure he liked the burst of pleasure her calling him Uncle Connor brought. He'd been on his own for a lot of years. Too many to get caught up in family ties at this point.

"Do you like school?" he asked, trying to make conversation. What did adults talk to kids about?

"Yes. My bestest friends are in my class. And Mrs. Webb is my favorite teacher. I get to be class helper next week. And in March, I'm going to be Student of the Week!"

"Wow, sounds impressive." He brushed the snow off the door of his rented SUV and opened it. Boosting her up into the high cab, he was surprised at how little she weighed. There was a lot about children he didn't know. The lack had never bothered him before.

"So which way?" Connor asked as he came to the driveway. Angie directed him toward the school.

"You walk this far?" he asked as they quickly covered the blocks.

"When I lived with Mommy and Daddy, Mommy would drive me. But Jenny lives closer, so I can walk."

"She doesn't drive you?" Angie seemed too little to him to be out wandering the streets all by herself. Though as he looked around, he noticed there were several groups of children trudging through the snow, some playing around, others trying to ignore snowballs winging their way.

"Not unless it's raining. She doesn't walk too good and doesn't like to drive."

"What?"

"Because of her hurt leg."

"She hurt her leg?" He hadn't noticed anything wrong. But, come to think of it, he hadn't seen her walking.

"What happened?"

"She was in a car crash. That's my school. There's my friend Cilla." Angie was so excited she almost opened the door before Connor pulled to a stop. He reached out to grab her.

"Wait until I park."

"Hurry up, Uncle Connor. We have time to play on the swings before the bell rings."

Once released from the car, she took off running without a backward look.

So much for Uncle Connor, he thought wryly. He leaned against the SUV, crossing his arms over his chest and watched the children for a few moments. The shrill shrieks, laughter and yelling would drive him crazy in no time. How did teachers stand it?

"Can I help you?"

Connor looked to his right, and came face to face with a harridan.

"Are you the school principal?" he asked, making a lucky guess.

She nodded regally.

He held out his hand. "I'm Connor Wolfe, Angie Benson's uncle. I'd like to meet Mrs. Webb, if I might."

Jenny was working on the Inn's accounts in the late morning, the office door standing wide, when she caught a glimpse of Connor entering through the heavy glass doors.

He'd been gone for hours. What had he been doing?

She quickly lowered her gaze to the numbers and tried to ignore her increased pulse rate. She'd spent more time thinking about the man since she'd sat down to work than was wise. He was here for Angie, nothing more.

Not that she would allow herself to become caught up in more—especially with someone like him even if he made overtures—which he had not.

"Got a minute?" He filled the doorway.

She caught her breath and nodded, trying to slow her heart beat which had racheted up another notch. He looked tired, more so than when he'd arrived. And the sadness in the depth of his eyes hadn't abated. Was it because of Cathy's untimely death? Regrets for things that could never be changed now that death had intervened?

She knew how that went. Pushing away the old familiar ache, she tried to smile. No one else was interested in her own personal ghosts.

"What can I help you with?"

He pulled up the chair and sat where he'd sat last night. "I met Mrs. Webb. She looks like a strict teacher, but Angie seems to like her.''

''She adores her. And she's excellent.''

''Don't tell me you had her, too,'' he said slowly, a cocky smile touching the corners of his lips.

''No, but her reputation is excellent.''

''And I thought everyone had been here since the dawn of time. What about tradition? What happened to your third grade teacher?''

''She retired a number of years ago. Still lives in Rocky Point, though.'' She didn't mind his gentle teasing. It might help him to find an outlet for the anguish he must feel at Cathy's death. She knew how it felt. There had been no easy outlet for her when her father died. Only guilt and regret.

''I stopped by the sheriff's office again. He gave me the lawyer's name. So I went to see him.''

Jenny nodded. She should have told him Jeb Morris was Harrison's attorney.

''He said basically everything they had was left to Angie. The insurance will cover the mortgage payoff of the house with a little left over. He can sell the fishing boat, liquidate assets and invest for her. It isn't as if there is any personal property after the fire.''

''She has her teddy bear. She'd taken it with her when she went to spend the night at Cilla's.''

''If she hadn't done that, she'd have been killed, too, right?''

Jenny nodded. The shock of the propane tank explosion and consequent fire still unsettled her. And but for Cilla having Angie over, the little girl would have died that night as well.

Connor rubbed his face with one hand, rose and paced back and forth. ''It's a hell of a thing. I hadn't seen Cathy in years. Not since she got married, actually, though we spoke on the phone once or twice. But I never expected not to have her around all my life.''

''Take care of her daughter, that's the best you can do now,'' Jenny said gently, almost liking him by his display of vulnerability. He was a man hurting for the loss of his sister. Maybe feeling sad that he hadn't tried harder to keep in contact. That chance was forever gone.

''I can see to Angie's welfare.'' He sat again, leaned closer to the desk. ''Her attorney said we could use the proceeds of the investment for her support if needed. I have plenty, so I'd rather invest that for her future, when she's an adult. Support won't be an issue, if that was worrying you.''

''Me? Why should it bother me? Oh, you mean for a prospective family who might agree to take her in?'' Jenny asked.

''I think you should keep her. You two already get on, she depends on you. She seems settled in here. You already have a routine down pat.''

Jenny grew quiet. She didn't like the trend of the conversation. She'd love to have Angie stay with her, but it would never work. She knew that. It was enough to have to face the reality. She didn't want to have to spell it out to a stranger.

''I can't.''

''You said that, but if money was an issue, I'm telling you it's not. I can afford whatever you need.''

''It's not the money. She's welcome here as long as she wants. I have enough to take care of her.''

''Then what? A boyfriend who doesn't like kids?'' Connor demanded.

She shook her head. ''No boyfriend.'' She should be so lucky to have one special relationship. She had plenty of activities, friends. She would not tempt fate by wishing for more.

"Then what?"

"I just can't. Please leave it at that."

Connor jumped to his feet again, paced the small office. "You would be the best choice," he said. "She likes you, that's obvious. She's comfortable here. Has her friends. What's the problem?"

"You've been here less than twenty-four hours. You just met Angie, just met me. You don't know us or anything about us. If you don't want to take her home with you to L.A., then give me time to see if there might be someone in town who would take her. Don't you think you should give that option a chance?"

"I didn't make it big in my business by not recognizing opportunities and acting on them!" he said, turning back to lean over the desk. "And I see a good one right here."

She stared up at him, her eyes wide, her lips parted slightly. Connor almost groaned. He was angry, but that anger was changing slightly the longer he stared into her dark blue eyes.

He wanted her!

Dammit he didn't need this complication. He was here for his niece, not some toss in the hay with an uptight, prissy inn keeper.

She pushed herself up, leaned on the desk and glared at him. ''I said no. Let it drop!''

Only a few inches separated them. He could lean closer so easily and touch those soft lips. For a moment time stood still.

CHAPTER THREE

HE WAS going to kiss her! Jenny was stunned, mesmerized, unable to move a muscle as his eyes gazed into hers. The anger faded, awareness took hold. Blood rushed through her, heating her until she thought it was high summer. The silence stretched out between them, slowly his eyes narrowed and he leaned just a bit closer.

She couldn't allow it. She'd just met the man. She didn't know him, he didn't know her. It had been years since anyone kissed her. She didn't want this!

Curiosity took hold. What would it be like?

Her leg ached, her knees grew weak, her whole body trembled.

She pulled back as if dashed with cold water. What was she doing? The man was a stranger—

Her heart raced as if she'd been in a marathon. She tried to pull some semblance of normalcy around her, but couldn't think of a single clever thing to say. He had not been about to kiss her. Did he suspect she thought he would? If he laughed, she didn't know what she'd do.

He straightened and ran one hand through his hair, his frustration obvious.

"I have some phone calls to make to California. Can you give me directions to Cathy's place? I want to see it later."

Jenny nodded. She wanted him to leave, needed to be alone to try to regain her equilibrium. But something made her say, "I have some errands to run this afternoon. If you wish, I can show you where they lived. And take you to the cemetery."

She couldn't believe she'd offered. She should be putting as much distance between them as she could. She didn't even like the man. How could she entertain fantasies about him *kissing* her?

Connor glanced at his watch and nodded once. "If I finish the calls before you leave, I'll take you up on it."

She sat down slowly, amazed she'd been able to stand so long on knees that felt like cooked spaghetti. "One o'clock then. If you're ready fine, if not then I can leave the directions at the front desk."

"Either way." He turned and headed out, stopping at the open door to look back at her. Jenny thought he'd say something more, but he glanced at her mouth, shook his head and continued on.

Once he left, reality asserted itself. She shook off her unusual mood and forced herself to study the latest expenditures. The last man in the world she should ever day-dream about was Connor Wolfe.

Promptly at one o'clock, Jenny walked into the lobby. Glancing around for Connor, she smiled at the woman behind the desk. "I'm off to do some errands. I'll be back by the time Angie gets home from school."

"Take your time. I'll be here if you're not. She'll be fine. You be careful, it's slippery out there. I almost fell coming in this morning," Libby said.

Jenny nodded. She always took care when walking in the snow, not daring to risk a fall. She double-checked the time and then shrugged. Maybe Connor had changed his mind. Or maybe his phone calls weren't completed. She took a pad and wrote down the directions clearly. Rocky Point wasn't large, he could find the lot easily enough.

She refused to admit feeling disappointed he wouldn't be joining her.

She headed outside to her Jeep. The freshly fallen snow sparkled in the sunshine. The bright blue sky was cloudless. The air was frigid, hanging in little puffs around her mouth when she breathed. Her cheeks tingled with the cold. It was beautiful, but she didn't like it. What wouldn't she give to live in Key West, Florida! It was as far south as the continental U.S. extended and she wished she lived there every winter.

Max had cleared the steps and the walkway. Her handyman was invaluable all year long, but he took extra care removing snow and keeping the walkways ice free. Her cane never slipped once on her slow way to the car which he had also cleaned off. She slid behind the wheel and shut the door, grateful to have made it safely. Starting the engine, she backed slowly out. Turning to head through the parking lot for the street, she was startled by the rap on the side window.

She stopped short. Connor stood by the passenger door. She unlocked it and he slipped in.

"When you say one, you mean one," he commented.

"I thought you were still on the phone," she said as she pulled out onto the quiet street and headed for the other side of town.

"I took care of emergencies. I have a good staff. Anything they can't handle can wait." Connor stared out the window as they drove through the several blocks of stores and businesses that comprised downtown Rocky Point. The main street led to the water, where rows of piers jutted into the Atlantic, several fishing boats bobbing in the quiet cove. The rest were out trawling.

They swept around the bend and headed along the coast road.

"Harrison was a fisherman," Connor said.

"I know. I knew him most of my life. He was a few years older, but his family had lived here for generations."

"Hard life."

"Harder than some, not as dangerous as others. He liked it. His father and grandfather had been fishermen. They both died in a storm a number of years ago. I guess Harrison always thought he'd die at sea."

"Are your parents around?"

She shook her head. "My mother died when I was a baby, my father when I was a teenager."

"Was he also a fisherman?" he asked.

Jenny flicked him a quick glance. "He was a mechanic. He worked on the boats sometimes, cars the rest of the time."

"Did you inherit the Inn from him?"

She shook her head again.

"He couldn't have been very old. But at least he didn't risk his life and limb battling the North Atlantic. It's odd, but when Cathy first told me about Harrison, I pictured her a widow before she was thirty. I never expected—"

"It's coming up," she said softly. Turning onto Turnbull Road, she slowed then stopped. Snow covered the ruins, a foundation and forlorn chimney rising to the sky. A couple of blackened trees remained as lonely sentinels to the house that had once stood in the center of the lot. Demolition crews had cleared away the debris. Only the foundation remained, now blanketed by the white snow. Behind where the house once stood a swing set sat in isolation. Beyond, a handful of trees and a small meadow. The snow covered all, giving a sparkling shroud to what once had been a happy home.

"Nothing remained," Jenny said sadly. "By the time the fire department arrived, the entire structure was blazing. Nothing was saved, not the car, not any clothes, pictures, china. Or the people."

He stared at the spot, his jaws clenched tightly. Jenny longed to offer sympathy, to do something that would ease the pain of loss. There was really nothing she could do. She didn't know this man, didn't know what might help.

But she had to try. She could almost feel his pain, or was it an echo of her own?

"She was happy. She loved Harrison, adored Angie."

"She should have had another fifty years."

"Yes, they both should have. And Angie should have had her parents until she grew up. But life doesn't always work that way."

He was silent for a moment, then looked at Jenny. "Shall we go to the cemetery?"

In only a few moments, Jenny slowly turned in through the arched stone gate of the Rocky Point Cemetery and stopped.

The road winding through the cemetery had not been ploughed.

"I don't want to risk getting stuck. See that tree over there," she pointed to the right. "They are buried about twenty feet beyond it. There's no stone. One's not been commissioned yet. The plot is next to the Burford's stone."

He opened the door and climbed out. Jenny watched as he wove his way through the monuments and headstones, tramping in the snow, glancing at each headstone as he walked, until he stopped. Maybe he'd commission a tombstone for them. Angie talked about it when Jenny brought her. A marker should be made for her parents. If Connor didn't want to, Jenny would. Cathy had been her dearest friend.

A few minutes later he headed back, walking with his head down, his eyes still glancing here and there at the different tombstones. He stopped for a moment and read one, then moved on.

When he got back into the Jeep he looked at her. "Was Samuel Gordon your father?"

She nodded.

"You were young when he died."

"Nineteen," she said clamping down on the old ache.

"It must have been hard for you."

"At least I was older than Angie," she said shortly. "I have some errands to do, shall I drop you back at the Inn?"

"Where are you going?"

"To the printers to check on the proofs for a new brochure, and then to the college to go over the plans for a dinner they wish to have catered during February Festival."

"February Festival? What's that?"

"An annual, winter festival sponsored by the college, but held throughout the town. There're ice sculpture competitions, light parades, and booths selling everything from hot chocolate to sun beads. The college suspends classes encouraging the students to participate. The ice sculptures are fantastic, some can take days to make. It's a big tourist draw. One of the alumni groups is having a dinner which we're catering."

"I'll ride shotgun. I'm in no hurry to get back to the Inn—until Angie returns. And I wanted to see the college where Cathy went."

"We'll beat Angie home," Jenny promised.

As she drove to the printer's she tried to ignore Connor. Maybe she should have insisted she drop him at the Inn. He seemed to fill the space in the Jeep, taking more room than seemed warranted. She was conscious of his wide shoulders, of how tall he sat, his head almost brushing the roof. His legs could have used more room, but he had the seat all the way back.

She tried to concentrate on her driving, but it was difficult since her attention remained on Connor. He seemed totally unaware of her. What did she expect? She was not someone to inspire passion in men.

Jenny turned into the parking lot by the printer's, studying the cleared space with some dismay. It was a haphazard job. Why couldn't everyone take as much care as Max did?

She parked as close to the store as she could, but there would still be fifty feet or more to navigate before safely reaching the front door. She stared at the slick parking lot, trying to gauge just how she'd cross it.

"Is there a problem?" Connor asked when she made no move to get out of the car.

Oh God, she hadn't even thought about Connor. She closed her eyes for a moment then opened them. Any thoughts of possible kisses just died.

''No, no problem.'' Did he even know she used a cane? Wouldn't that be the perfect turnoff. Once he saw her staggering along, he'd want nothing to do with her. A man who vacationed in Tahiti could have his choice of women. Why look twice as a staid innkeeper who walked with a cane?

She took a resolute breath and opened the car door, reaching for the hated device. Slowly she eased out of the Jeep, until she had her balance on the pavement. She stepped away, closing the door behind her.

She heard him get out of the car and walk on the crunchy snow. She couldn't do more than notice, she had to concentrate on where to step, and how to keep her weight evenly distributed to minimize a chance of falling. She didn't want to see the pity in his gaze, or the distaste.

''Need any help?'' he asked, stopping beside her.

''I can manage.''

They walked in silence for several steps. She skidded slightly, recovered. At least he didn't grab her.

''Angie said you had hurt your leg in a car crash, what happened?''

"A drunk driver hit us broadside."

"Recently?"

"When I was nineteen."

"Is that when your father died?" he asked.

"Same time. He wasn't in the crash, however."

They had reached the door. With a soft sigh of relief, Jenny stepped inside.

"Hi, Jenny, I have those proofs." Old Hiram Mawlings smiled at her from behind the cluttered counter that separated the narrow entry way from the printing concern. The big machines took up most of the floor space, with drafting tables near the windows for design work. Boxes of paper were stacked against one wall.

The old iron printers had long ago been replaced with computer driven ones, but the smell of oil and ink still lingered in the shop.

Hiram looked at Connor curiously.

"Hiram, this is Connor Wolfe, Angie's uncle," Jenny said.

"I heard they finally tracked you down. Glad to see you came right away. Terrible tragedy. I'm sorry for your loss."

"Thank you," Connor said. He stood quietly beside Jenny when Hiram pulled out a folder and showed her the layout of the new brochure. He leaned over her shoulder to study the design.

She looked up, right into his dark eyes. He was so close she could feel his breath brush against her cheek. So close she could almost feel his lips touching hers. Too close, she thought.

Jenny jerked away. She did not need to become infatuated with some stranger who didn't want to stay a minute longer in Rocky Point than he had to. Now was not the time for her imagination to take over. Remain focused, she chided herself.

"Looks good," he said. "May I?" He reached out and picked up the text portion, skimming through it. He put it down and looked at her. "Reads good. Did you write it?"

"I did, young man. By this time, I ought to know what I'm doing," Hiram said testily, moving the folder away from Connor and glancing back at Jenny.

"Any changes? Otherwise we can go to press," Hiram said.

"It looks great, as always, Hiram. Thank you."

"I'll have them ready before the Festival. You can distribute them all over."

"That's the plan."

"You booked up?" Hiram asked.

"Every room spoken for. It'll be hectic, but a real boost to the bottom line."

"Is every year." He looked at Connor suspiciously. "You staying long?"

"Long enough to decide what to do about Angie," he said evenly.

"What's to decide? She's your niece, take her home and love her up a storm. Won't make up for losing her folks, but it'll help," Hiram said.

"I'll keep that under advisement," Connor said, a hint of amusement in his tone.

Knowing the tension would only increase the longer the two men faced off, Jenny wanted to leave before Hiram got his back up and made things worse. Or Connor said something that would spark an argument.

"Call me when the job's done and I'll pick it up," she said with a warm smile.

"You might want to clear your parking lot better when you do. Someone could fall," Connor said.

"Shh," Jenny hissed, turning to leave.

Connor opened the door for her and held it as she walked through.

"He needs to clear it. Why deny it? It's a lawsuit waiting to happen," Connor said.

"He does it himself and gets testy if people complain."

"So?"

She paused and looked up at him. He seemed so much taller standing beside her like that. Dressed all in black, he looked intimidating. And foreign in the snowy setting with his dark tan, his rugged good looks. The aura of confidence and assurance seemed to envelop her. She wished she could tap into some of that confidence to know exactly how to handle the man and his intentions for Angie.

"So he has his pride. He wants to do a good job, but he isn't as young as he used to be," she said. Wasn't it obvious?

"So you adopt old folks as well as orphans?"

She didn't deign to answer. Hiram had been kind to her long ago, she didn't forget.

They walked slowly back to the Jeep. He opened her door for her, watching as she maneuvered into the driver's seat. Jenny felt self-conscious in a way she hadn't felt in years. She wished he wouldn't watch her so closely. Hadn't he ever seen a disabled person before?

Maybe not. With his athletic prowess, he probably didn't cross paths with those less mobile.

She wished she could be free and whole again. That she could still move with the grace and suppleness and stamina she'd once taken for granted. For years she'd accepted the way things were, but his arrival made her yearn for what couldn't be.

"I'll drop you at the Inn," she said when they headed out of town.

"I want to see the college," he countered.

"Why?"

"Cathy took some classes there. I'd like to see the place."

"It's not big like UCLA or USC. And it doesn't have a lot of prestige behind it. We're proud to have it here, however. It revitalized the town when it was built about forty years ago. Fishing has been declining over the last few generations."

"It's a small liberal arts college, I know, I read the brochure you have in the rooms. I'd like to see it. Let's hope they did a better job of clearing their parking lot," he said sardonically.

She bristled. "I managed fine."

"You are not the only person to use that parking lot. What if someone fell?"

He was right, she was being overly sensitive. What if someone like Mrs. Wellborn fell—she was eighty if she was a day. Or Betsy Funchess—six months pregnant and starting to move awkwardly. Hiram should have cleared it better. Or hired one of the college kids.

Connor walked around the campus while Jenny settled the assignment with the alumni office. He was waiting by the Jeep when she came out, arms crossed, head tilted back to catch the sun. It was still cold, but the dark cloth probably trapped whatever heat the sun generated.

"Nice place," he said as they headed back toward the Inn.

She suspected a hint of patronizing condescension in his tone. Jenny didn't answer, telling herself it didn't matter what he thought of Rocky Point or Blackstone College.

"Angie will be home soon. She will want to go out ice skating as soon as she changes," she said to change the topic.

"Likes the sport, huh?"

"Try crazy about it."

"Does the town have a rink?"

"Not really. There's a vacant lot beyond the Inn's property that's flooded every winter for people to skate. Safer than a pond, no depth when it melts. But it provides endless hours of fun for the kids."

"Is she any good at it?"

"I don't know. I've never seen her skate."

"Why not?"

Why not? Because of the memories. Because of the regrets. Because of the anguish of what might have been. But she didn't tell him that.

"It's too hard for me to walk to the rink through the snow and dirt." That was an answer that didn't bring forth any question in return.

"Her friends skate?"

"Most of them. You'll meet her two best friends today, Andy and Cilla."

"Brother and sister?"

"No, Andy is an only child. Cilla is one of eight."

"Eight! People still have families that large?" He looked at her. "How many do you plan to have when you get married?"

Jenny had never thought about having a family. She'd been too driven when younger. Then, after the accident, she knew her chances of ever finding a man to marry her were slim. She had her Inn to give her purpose.

And for a few months, she'd had Angie. Her heart squeezed when she thought of the little girl leaving. If she moved to Los Angeles, would Jenny ever see her again?

"I don't plan to marry," she replied as the silence stretched out.

"So are either of these families ones you think might take Angie?" he asked.

She turned on the blinker and eased into the Inn's parking lot. "Andy's parents might consider it. I doubt Eve Hanley wants another child with eight of her own."

"Have you called to feel them out?"

She stopped and looked at him. "Not yet. Are you sure you want to do this? Think of Angie for a moment. You are her only living relative. If you don't take her, she'll view it as rejection."

"Why? She never knew me. And if she loves ice skating, L.A. is the last place she should be. If we go the boarding school route, I could have Stephie look for something in New England."

"Who's Stephie?"

"My secretary."

Jenny was quiet for a moment, then asked, "How did you feel when your mom left?"

Connor looked at her for a moment. "It wasn't the same thing."

"Close. Blood ties are important. To sever them gives rise to feelings that can't be explained away logically. Angie needs you."

"She needs a woman's influence, not a bachelor uncle. Why don't you keep her? She's happy here, that much is obvious. If it's the money—"

"No, it's not money. I have plenty of money. It's about all I do have." Jenny opened the door and climbed out. Before she'd taken two steps, Connor stopped her, turning her to face him, careful not to unbalance her.

"If you won't take her, then call the whoever you think might take her on, but I can't stay here indefinitely. This has to be resolved soon."

"Stay until you get to know her better. She's lonely, and sad and trying to make the best of things." Jenny wished she could make him see how much he could do for his niece.

"I'm not changing my mind. I can't take care of a kid."

"Just get to know her, spend some time with her, do things with her. She's a great little girl."

He weighted the options. Jenny could almost see the wheels spinning in his mind. Finally he looked deep into her eyes.

"On the condition you help build the bridge."

"You don't need me."

"That's the condition. If things shake out, maybe I'll see about other arrangements. But in the meantime, call Andy's parents."

"What other arrangements?" she asked warily.

"I don't know yet. But I'm not set up to watch a child. I travel a lot. I don't have time for family ties."

"Give Angie a chance."

"You know the condition. Yes or no?"

"Fine! I'll see what I can do." She turned and headed for the front porch of the Inn, emotions jumbling around. She was mad, and intrigued, and just the tiniest bit pleased he wanted her help. And if it kept Angie in Rocky Point for a while longer, so much the better—for both of them.

Connor watched her go, almost seeing waves of anger shimmering around her. He waited until she was hidden from view before relaxing his stance. If she had slipped, he would have dashed to her rescue.

Like she was coming to his?

He didn't need rescuing. He agreed to spend a little time with Angie, no hardship. He'd call Stephanie and let her know his stay would be extended a few more days.

Somehow he would figure out how to get Jenny to agree to his plan. She and Angie were perfect together. Why couldn't she see it? There had to be some pressure he could bring to bear. What was Jenny Gordon's weakness?

CHAPTER FOUR

JENNY was in the kitchen reviewing the plans for the catered dinner with Sally Thompson when Angie rushed in later that afternoon.

"Hi Jenny, I'm home. Can I go skating?" The child almost danced with impatience.

"Do you have a lot of home work?"

"No, only spelling and one page in math. I can do it after dinner."

"Okay. Dress warmly."

"You always say that. Is Uncle Connor still here? He was going to watch me skate."

"I believe he is. Try room seven."

"Okay, bye." She dashed out again.

"If we could only bottle that energy," Sally Thompson said wistfully.

"I know what you mean." For Jenny, she wanted simpler things—just to walk normally would be nice. To run again, to skate. She sighed softly and turned her attention back to the task at hand. Might as well wish for the moon. Things would never go back to the way they had been.

She and Mrs. Thompson were just about finished when Angie and Connor entered. Angie had changed into warmer clothes and had her skates over her shoulder. She almost danced into the kitchen.

"Guess what, Jenny, Uncle Connor says you can go with us to see me skate. You've never seen me, you'll be so proud of what I can do!"

Jenny looked at Connor in dismay. "I can't go."

"Sure you can. I'll help you."

"This isn't a walk in a cleared parking lot. The ground between here and the skating rink is covered in snow, uneven beneath it. It's out of the question. I don't think you should have even suggested it." Anger and embarrassment warred. She'd told him earlier why she hadn't seen Angie skate, why had he brought it up?

"If it gets too rough for you, I'll carry you," he said.

For a moment pictures from the past jumped to mind. Karl holding her above his head, sweeping her up onto his shoulders, holding her as they spun.

She looked at Connor, stunned at the picture that superseded the others in her mind. Her carried in his arms like Rhett had carried Scarlett—held close to that muscular chest. His face and hers close together, her arms locked around his neck.

"I think that sounds like a fine idea," Sally Thompson said beaming at Connor. "Nice of you to offer young man."

"It's a dumb idea and I'm not going," Jenny snapped.

"Oh, Jenny, please come. You've never seen me skate close up. And Uncle Connor can carry you, he's strong. He lifted me up into the car this morning with no trouble at all."

"Can't get a better testimonial than that," he said. Leaning closer, he whispered, "Dare you."

"Oh, like that's going to get me to go," she said, almost laughing. For a wistful instant she thought about saying yes.

"Come on, Jenny. You will love seeing me skate," Angie implored. "Please! Walt cleared off the snow and added some water, so it's smooth. Maybe I can do my spin and you'd get to see me."

"Don't want to miss a spin," Connor said, his eyes narrowed as he studied

Jenny. "If you don't think I can carry you, we can take the car. It'll go through the snow."

"You can't drive a car over the ground even if it wasn't covered in snow, too many kids around."

"Then trust me to get you there in one piece."

Sally urged her, Angie pleaded. Finally Jenny capitulated.

"Let me get some really warm clothes on, first, however. I don't want to freeze to death halfway there," she said, stalling.

"I'll see you don't freeze," Connor said.

Jenny almost asked how he planned to do that, but discretion proved wiser. She could warm herself up with the fantasies that had filled her head last night when she should have been falling asleep.

They had barely started for the rink when Jenny knew it was a master mistake. She had slipped twice, wrenching her hip once and couldn't find a place her cane didn't skid.

Angie ran on ahead. Soon sitting on one of the benches that encircled the skating rink, she began to don her skates.

"This isn't going to work," Jenny said hoping she could make it back to the Inn.

"Then we go to plan B," Connor said, scooping her up easily and holding her against his chest.

Taken by surprise, Jenny flung her arm around his neck. "Put me down, Connor. You can't carry me."

But he was already doing so, striding across the snowy field as if they were strolling along a cleared sidewalk. Sure-footed and strong, he never faltered.

"Relax. You're helping me keep warm. It seems colder every time I step outside. Why people live here is beyond me."

For penance, she almost said. That was her reason. She couldn't speak for the entire town, of course. But she wisely kept silent.

In no time they reached the rink and he slowly released her until she stood on her two feet, balanced on the packed snow.

Kids were skating by, waving at friends, yelling, laughing. Taking two small steps, she sank down on one of the benches and watched. Angie plunged onto the ice and skated feverishly around twice, then stopped near where Connor and Jenny sat.

"Did you see me?" she called.

"You are doing great!" Jenny called, delighted to see the happiness in the child's eyes. It was nice after the sadness normally there.

"Try your spin." For a moment the old longing rose so strongly Jenny thought it would knock her over. She had loved skating at Angie's age. Loved feeling the freedom on the ice, the cold wind against her cheeks, the sensation of speeding along so fast no one could catch her.

"Okay, watch me," Angie said.

Watch me, Daddy, Jenny's voice echoed down the years.

She blanked the past out. Focused on Angie.

Connor stretched out his long legs, crossed his arms across his chest—a favorite pose, or was he trying to keep warm? Jenny didn't ask. They still had the walk home. He'd have to carry her again. Feeling like an idiot, she wished she could make it under her own steam, but knew it was impossible. Still, better to be indignant to be so dependent than to give into the feelings that rushed through her when held in his arms.

Angie spun slowly, then straightened and promptly fell.

Jenny wanted to reach out to help her. That was the hard part, spinning so fast her equilibrium was off, then skating in a straight line into the next move. She remembered the endless practices until she got it right. She remembered the elation when she succeeded.

"She's a trouper," Connor said, watching Angie. "Every time she falls, she gets back up right away."

"It's a part of learning." Jenny wished she could get on the ice and give her pointers. Show her how to balance, how to latch onto something on the horizon and skate toward it when coming out of a spin. But she was never going on the ice again.

Angie got tired of practicing her spins, and falling, and began to skate around, forward and backward, joining in with her friends. She laughed with Cilla, and played crack the whip with a group of children.

"Is she better than the other kids?" Connor asked at one point.

"They're all out to have fun." Jenny's defenses rose instinctively.

"I never said they weren't. But she seems to have better control than some of the other kids. Maybe she should be in competition."

"Just like a man. Leave her alone. She likes skating for skating's sake." That's how it had started for her. She didn't want Angie to get caught up in competition. Let her enjoy her sport.

"What does that crack mean?" His interested shifted from Angie to Jenny.

"Just because someone is good at something doesn't mean they have to compete somewhere. Let her enjoy her delight in skating without the pressure to perform. Guys always make a contest out of things."

"And you speak from experience."

Jenny realized the pitfalls. She shrugged, "General observation," she said. She shivered, growing colder. It was getting late and before long the sun would be gone. Already the temperature had dropped several degrees.

"I'd like to go back now," she said, standing. She beckoned to Angie.

When the child stopped near the edge of the ice, she looked at Jenny, Connor now standing beside her.

"Are you leaving?"

"We aren't keeping warm by skating a hundred miles an hour," Jenny said. "You are doing great. I'm glad I got to see you. Keep practicing the spins, you'll get them."

"I'll take Jenny back to the Inn and come back for you, okay, short stuff?"

"If you want, but I can get home by myself when Cilla and Andy leave." With a wave, Angie went to join her friends.

"I can try walking," she said, looking at the distance to the Inn. It would be impossible, but so would being held by Connor again. She never should have agreed to come to the rink.

"Relax, think about how you are really keeping me warm," he said, reaching over to pick her up again.

Holding her firmly against his chest, he looked at her. Jenny tried to hold herself apart, but it was a losing battle. Her arm was around his neck, her face only inches from his. The warmth she received from him was staggering. How did he keep so hot on such a cold afternoon?

"Thank you for bringing me," she said primly, her eyes not meeting his.

"But you hated every moment," he said as he strode across the field.

"I enjoyed seeing her skate. I've only see her from the porch of the Inn, and I can't even distinguish boys from girls at that distance. But I'm sorry to be such a bother."

"No bother."

"Oh, come on, Connor, lugging me around like a sack of cornmeal?"

He stopped in the middle of the field and didn't move until she chanced a glance at him. His face was hard, his eyes narrowed.

"I told you it was no bother. You may have hang-ups about your disability, but don't be calling me a liar." His voice was hard, his gaze implacable.

"I never said—"

"Telling me what I said wasn't so is calling me a liar and I resent the hell out of it," he said.

"I'm sorry." She swallowed. "I thought you were being polite."

He began walking again. "I'm not much on politeness, as you'll see the more you get to know me."

"I doubt I'll get to know you that much."

"Oh I don't know, you're still helping me with Angie, right? You'll get to see a lot of me over the next few days."

Jenny nodded, deflated slightly at the reminder. He wanted her help with Angie. There was no other reason for the two of them to be together.

At dinner time, Jenny suggested Angie

eat dinner with her uncle. "You need to get to know him better."

"I know him," Angie said. "I'd rather eat with you. What if he tells me we have to move to Los Angeles? I don't want to eat with him."

"He's your uncle, your next of kin. Your mother would have wanted him to take good care of you," Jenny replied, suspecting she would have to resort to other means to gain the child's compliance. Like offer to eat with them. Could she—eat that is, as aware of Connor as she was whenever near him?

"Mommy liked you. You two were bestest friends. I remember her telling Daddy. I want to stay with you," Angie said.

"Honey, I'm not a relative. Your uncle is."

"I don't care, I want to stay with you." Angie was becoming upset, her voice more shrill.

"Let's table that discussion," Jenny said. "How about we both eat with Uncle Connor?"

Angie seemed to consider it carefully, then nodded. "Okay. In the dining room?"

"Why not, it's certainly not crowded. And I think Uncle Connor would like it better than squeezing into our suite, don't you?''

Angie nodded. "Besides, the dining room will be all crowded when the February Festival starts so we won't be able to do it then," she said wisely. "But it will be good that it's busy."

Jenny laughed sadly. She could almost hear Cathy say the same words. She missed her friend so much. Angie promised to grow more and more like her mother as she grew up. Jenny wished she could watch all the stages.

Connor stood near the fireplace in the large reception area when they slowly descended the stairs a few minutes later. He turned to study them as they drew closer. Jenny was self-conscious, but Angie didn't appear to be, skipping the last few steps and racing over to him.

"Hi, Uncle Connor. Guess what, we get to eat in the dining room tonight. And Jenny is eating with us. Mostly we eat in our quarters, but since the Inn isn't crowded yet, we can eat in the dining room."

"Sounds like a treat," Connor said gravely, his gaze on Jenny.

Feeling flustered, she glanced around the

welcoming room to make sure everything was in order. She knew her job running the Inn. She was totally out of her depths with Connor Wolfe.

Angie chatted away during the meal, prompted by Jenny, easing the tension a bit. Jenny tried to ignore Connor's presence, but found it impossible. Every time she glanced his way, she found his gaze fixed on her.

She wished he'd focus on Angie. She was the reason he was here, after all. Every time Angie fell silent, Jenny suggested a new topic for her to explain to her uncle.

Did all children have trouble finding topics to discuss at mealtime? Angie usually talked more than she ate when it was just the two of them. Being around Connor hadn't quite worked out the way she thought it would. Angie hadn't warmed up to him like Jenny had hoped.

His talk of boarding school hadn't helped, she was sure.

Jenny was almost finished her entrée when Jason, the night desk clerk, came into the dining room. Spotting Jenny, he headed directly for her.

''Sorry to interrupt dinner, but Sheriff Tucker is out front wanting to speak to you,

Jenny,'' he said, glancing at Connor and then back to Jenny.

''Is there a problem?'' she asked, placing her napkin beside her place and rising. As always, it took her a moment to get her joints working properly, and to deal with the pain.

''I don't think so. He just wanted to speak with you,'' Jason said.

Jenny smiled at Angie. ''Finish telling your uncle about the spelling bee. I'll be back after I've seen the sheriff.''

Once standing, she gripped her cane and headed for the lobby.

''Hi, Isaac, is anything wrong?'' Jenny asked when the older man turned to greet her.

''No. I'm on my way home and had some information I wanted to pass along before morning. I'm not taking you away from anything, am I?''

She shook her head and led the way near the fireplace. It was still cold and windy outside. Even though the Inn was weather tight, she still felt as if she were chilled.

''Angie doing okay with her new uncle?'' he asked when Jenny indicated he should take a seat. She eased down into a ladder-back chair.

"She's a bit shy around him. And he's not doing that much to remedy the situation." She wouldn't start in on her views of his plans for boarding school. She still had hopes they could find an alternative that would be best for Angie.

"I may have another solution."

"What?"

"We've turned up her grandfather."

"Cathy's father?" Her friend never talked about her father. Jenny had thought he was dead.

"He's flying in tomorrow, anxious to see his granddaughter. Maybe she and he will hit it off better than she has with Connor Wolfe."

"Don't you approve of Connor?" she asked, picking up undertones in Isaac's voice.

He shrugged. "A bit too arrogant for my tastes. I spoke with the grandfather on the phone a little while ago. He said he and Cathy had been estranged but he wanted to heal the breach."

"Where does he live?"

"San Diego."

Jenny felt for poor Angie. No matter what, it looked as if she was bound for California.

"So where does this leave Angie? Does one have a higher claim than the other?" she asked.

"I'm hoping they can work it out between them," Isaac said. "The grandfather sounds like he'd really love to have her live with him."

"And Connor doesn't," she murmured.

"So maybe there's no problem. He'll be here late tomorrow. I suggested he stay here, but he also asked about a motel, so I told him about the one out on the highway. Let me know if you need anything." He rose.

"Thanks for coming by, Isaac."

"Feel I owed you since you didn't get the message about Connor Wolfe." He gave a half salute and headed back outside.

Jenny remained in her seat for a while longer. The warmth from the fire felt good. She was stalling, she knew it, but for some reason she didn't want to return to the dinner table. She'd eaten enough.

How would Angie take the news? Apparently she didn't know she had a grandfather any more than she'd known about her uncle. What would Cathy have wanted? Jenny wished Cathy and Harrison had made formal provisions for their daughter in the event of their death. It would have made things easier. Maybe they hadn't wished either relative to take Angie.

Poor Cathy, she certainly had not enjoyed a very close family. Jenny was glad Harrison had been so devoted. She knew her friend had loved him deeply and together they'd had a wonderful life.

Angie came into the lobby and crossed over to Jenny. "I don't like Uncle Connor," she announced, darting a dark look toward the dining room.

"Oh, and why is that?" Jenny asked, wondering what had gone on after she left.

"He's mean."

"How?" Jenny's instincts rose. If he were mean, she'd make sure—

"He said I couldn't have dessert because I didn't eat my broccoli. I said I could too and he said no."

Jenny hid a smile. If that was as mean as Connor ever got, Angie was one lucky girl. "You know you are to eat vegetables to grow up strong and smart."

"I don't like broccoli."

Connor strode out into the lobby, pausing a moment as he took in the picture of

Jenny sitting by the fire, Angie leaning trustingly against her.

Jenny looked up. Did Connor know how forbidding he could look with that dark scowl? Angie shrank closer to Jenny, watching Connor warily.

"I think you should go upstairs and start your homework," she said, giving the child a gentle pat. "I'll be up soon to check it and then you can take your bath."

"What about dessert?"

"I'm not going to countermand your uncle's edict," Jenny said firmly.

Angie scowled. "What does that mean, no dessert?"

"Right in one."

Angie dashed around Connor and raced up the stairs.

"You're good with her," he said, taking the ladderback chair next to Jenny's. He stretched his long legs out, tucking his hands into the pockets. He studied the fire for a moment. "I thought I'd have a mutiny when I said no dessert."

"I guess I've let her get away with a lot, trying to make up for the loss of her parents," Jenny said.

"I think you've hit a balance. Reconsider, Jenny Gordon. She'd do fine here and I'll pay enough for her upkeep.''

''It looks as if there'll be another option,'' she said, looking at him, struck again by the intensity he leashed. ''Isaac came to tell me they've located Angie's grandfather.''

Connor sat up at that. ''The devil you say! Angie is not going to go live with Brian Wolfe.''

''Is that his name? Isaac didn't say. He'll be here tomorrow. And why shouldn't she go with him? He's her grandfather.''

''How often did he visit Angie since she's been born?'' he said.

''About as often as you did,'' she retorted. ''I thought you'd be happy as a lark to have her off your hands. You don't want to take care of her, you wanted to shunt her off to some boarding school.''

''It's a hell of a lot better than putting her with Brian Wolfe. No.''

''No? Do you have that say? You were located as next of kin. Now she has someone else. Who, if Isaac's to be believed, really wants her to live with him.''

''Not unless there's some support money along with it, I can guarantee you that.''

''That's a terrible thing to say. You act

like her grandfather would only be interested in the money.''

''I've known the man all my life. Trust me, he isn't into family or doing good deeds. His sole function in life is to make money to support his lifestyle.''

''And yours isn't, I suppose!''

''Oh yes, I'm in it for the money. For lots of money. I'm never going hungry again, or have to wear clothes too small that make everyone laugh, or shoes with holes in them so my feet get soaked in the rain. You're damned straight on that one, Jenny Gordon, I'm in it for the money.''

But he wasn't, she thought. He'd offered to pay people to take care of Angie. He wasn't looking to make money off his niece.

She wasn't sure his father was, either. She hadn't met the man. She had only Connor's comments.

''When was the last time you saw your father?'' she asked.

''The day I turned eighteen. Fifteen years ago. And if I never saw him again, it would be too soon.'' He rose and crossed the lobby to the front door which he wrenched open and stepped outside.

Jenny was shocked at his statement.

She'd give anything to see her father again—if only for fifteen minutes.

Connor stood on the porch, taking in the cold air. He relished the feel of it cooling his temper. He had no business saying all he had to Jenny. Their family relationships were none of her concern. But the thought of his father flying in like a vulture to pick over the bones of Cathy's life had him furious. The old man had had nothing to do with him once he'd reached eighteen. You're old enough to make your own way, he'd told Connor. Their mother was living then, so Cathy still had a home. But when Evvie had died, Cathy had turned to him for a place to live—not their father.

She never would want her child to go to the old man. Why hadn't she put something in place to safeguard Angie?

The cold was chilling, the wind blew from the north. He took another breath, and tried to think logically. If nothing else, he owed it to his sister to take care of her child. Cathy had been the bright spot in his own life when younger. She had adored her older brother and tried so hard to fit in with his plans. When she couldn't, she went for her own dreams. And it looked as if she'd found them, for however short a time.

Looking up at the dark sky, he wondered if Cathy could see Angie now, see the mess things were in.

"I'll make sure he doesn't get her, Cath," he vowed aloud. "She will never have the kind of childhood we had."

CHAPTER FIVE

IT WAS late the next afternoon when Jenny first met Brian Wolfe. He arrived about the same time Connor had, but his entrance was totally different—he had a huge teddy bear in his arms. Jenny knew instantly who he was.

He looked around the reception area as he entered, missing nothing. She had come out to talk to Libby about the festivities the following week and watched him as he approached the desk.

"Howdy, lovely ladies. By chance is either of you Miss Jennifer Gordon? Brian Wolfe has come to claim his granddaughter." He plopped the teddy bear on the counter and beamed at both women.

Jenny smiled back. "I'm Jenny Gordon. Welcome to the Inn."

"Delighted to meet you. According to Sheriff Tucker, you're the angel who has been watching my dear granddaughter since the untimely demise of her parents."

For a moment, the smile left his face. "I can't believe my own little girl is no longer walking the earth." He paused a moment, then seemed to shake off his melancholia. "But I've been blessed with another generation. Where is my precious grandchild?"

"She's out skating right now. She'll be in soon. Or I can call her now if you like?" Jenny said. Brian reminded her of Harrison, friendly and outgoing. Quite a contrast with his son.

"If you wouldn't mind. I can't wait to meet her," Brian said.

Jenny nodded, already liking Brian Wolfe a lot more than she did his son. At least he seemed interested in Angie and anxious to meet her.

"I'll get her," Libby said, slipping from around the counter.

"Let's sit near the fire, it's cold out," Jenny invited, walking around the counter, leaning on her cane.

"Ah, dear lady, you've had an accident. Allow me," With a flourish, he offered his arm.

Jenny smiled and took it, but kept a grip on the cane. Gallantry was nice, but she relied on no one other than herself.

"It is cold here. I live in San Diego, where the weather is temperate year round," Brian commented as they approached the fire.

"Do you live near the water?"

"It's hard to be far from the ocean in that city. Does Angie like the sea?"

"It's too cold to swim here unless it's high summer and a hot day. But she swims well. Harrison and Cathy saw to that."

"Ah, yes. Harrison Benson. Tell me, Miss Gordon, did he make my daughter happy?"

"They were very happy," Jenny said.

He nodded, his eyes flicking toward the door.

"It'll take a minute or two for Libby to get Angie. Can I offer you something to drink? We have hot beverages for guests in the afternoon."

"Ah, now that you mention it, a shot of Scotch would be most welcome. It being so cold out and all."

Jenny nodded and rose. She'd thought he might want some hot cider or coffee or tea, but if he wanted scotch, she had it available. Not for customers, but for her own personal guests. It took only a moment to bring a glass from the small bar in her office.

Brian was sipping the drink when Angie and Libby entered.

Warily, Angie walked over to Jenny, her eyes on the man sitting beside her. Her glance moving on to the bear. Slowly her expression relaxed.

"Hello, love," Jenny said. "Look who's here." She had told Angie about her grandfather before bedtime last night.

"Angie Benson, this is Brian Wolfe, your mother's father."

"Hello," Angie said.

"It's like seeing Cathy at age eight," Brian said softly, his eyes studying the little girl. "Hello, granddaughter. I've brought you a teddy bear." He reached over for the bear and presented it to her.

"Thank you," Angie said with a smile.

"Sit with us and get acquainted," Brian said, patting the sofa beside him. "It's been a long time since I've had a little girl around. Your mother was a sweet child. I bet you are, too."

Jenny watched as the older man charmed Angie. What a difference between Brian and Connor. It looked as if the difficulties with Connor would be resolved—without looking for a family locally to keep Angie. If Brian had anything to do with it, she suspected Angie would be winging her way to San Diego before long.

"Ah, no, no snow. But we have skating rinks, where you can leave the hot summer weather outside and enjoy some ice time," he was saying.

Angie frowned. "It's not the same."

"No need to fret about that yet, child. We'll become best friends and decide what to do," Brian said. He sipped his drink and smiled genially at Jenny. "I appreciate your taking care of her until I could get here. Cathy and I lost touch, but I never stopped thinking about her."

Jenny nodded, trying to remember what Cathy had said about her father. Not much. Her friend had been reticent about her past. She had loved Harrison and Angie and relished living in Rocky Point. Jenny knew little beyond that. And she had never questioned it before. Now she wished she'd learned a bit more.

She had a hard time reconciling the pleasant man in front of her with the picture Connor had painted of his father. Was his view distorted? Had he deliberately maligned his father for some reason? She remembered his hostility when he'd thought she'd accused him of lying. Anything he said about his father, he believed.

"We start serving dinner in about fifteen minutes," Jenny said. "You'll join us, won't you, Brian?"

"Delighted, my dear. It'll give me more time to spend with Angie, and hear all about school and her friends."

"I'll let Sally know we'll be ready to eat at six."

Jenny rose and went into the kitchen, glancing back over her shoulder once before leaving the common area. Brian was listening attentively to Angie. The little girl hadn't totally warmed up to him, but her initial response was far better than with Connor.

Jenny would have to call Isaac later and thank him for persevering in finding more of Cathy's family. It looked as if this might be a good match for Angie.

The pang of sadness hit her as she moved through the dining room. She loved having Angie with her. She would miss her so much when she left—California was so far away.

When they moved into the dining room a little while later, Jenny wondered where

Connor was. She hadn't seen him all day. He had been angry last night learning about his father. Because of that, she'd expected him to confront the man when he first walked into the Inn. But there had been no sign of him.

Now his absence was beginning to worry her. From the little she knew of Connor, she'd expected a confrontation at the very least.

"This is a delightful place, my dear," Brian said as they sat down at a table for four. The only other occupied table was across the room, providing them with a sense of privacy.

"I wish you would consider staying here," Jenny invited graciously. "I have room until next week."

"The motel on the highway suits me fine. But I'll be over frequently to see Angie." He winked at the little girl. "Tomorrow I need to speak to the authorities."

Jenny nodded, studying Angie. The little girl was eating calmly. Suddenly she looked up, and became tense.

Jenny knew why before looking over her shoulder. She could sense the man entering. Meeting his gaze when she turned, she was again struck by his athletic body, his easy gait and air of authority. Dressed in black again. Didn't he have any other color in his wardrobe? She was shocked at the wave of awareness that swept through her. The snug pants outlined long legs, the black leather jacket enhanced the muscular build of his chest and shoulders—the arrogance made him look like every bad boy she'd ever heard about.

The dark glint in his eyes caught her attention. He looked from her to Brian and she could see the muscles in his jaw tighten.

He strode across the room as if he owned the place. Taking the vacant chair at the table he pulled it out and sat, his eyes never leaving his father.

"I didn't expect to see you here," he said evenly.

"Connor? Well, my boy, you have done well by yourself, by the looks of things," Brian smiled as his gaze assessed the gold watch on his son's wrist, the expensive leather jacket.

Jenny watched the two, feeling the tension rise. Suddenly she realized Brian's clothes were old, a bit worn. His hair could stand a trim. In comparison, Connor's clothing was obviously expensive and in good condition. His hair had been styled, not cut. Even his arrogance overshadowed Brian's charm.

"I came to claim my granddaughter," Brian said a bit testily. He reached for the glass of Scotch and finished the little remaining.

"I think not," Connor said.

"I'm glad you could join us," Jenny interposed, anxious to make sure things didn't get sticky. "After we eat, while Angie is doing her homework, maybe the three of us could meet in my office." The strong conviction in her voice penetrated. Both men looked at her in surprise. Brian then glanced at Connor. His dark eyes held Jenny's, then slowly he nodded.

"After dinner, then."

Angie looked warily at both men and then at Jenny for reassurance.

Poor child, Jenny thought. She needed to make sure Angie was taken care of, and let the two men fight their own battles when Angie wasn't around.

Dinner was strained. Jenny wondered if she could swallow anything, but tried to make things seem as normal as possible for Angie. Brian's charm diminished a little in the presence of his forbidding son. Jenny

wanted to kick Connor to make him be-
have. If he thought glaring at his father
throughout the meal was conducive to good
digestion, he had rocks in his head.

Finally Angie finished and looked at
Jenny. "Can I be excused. I have homework."

"Sure, sweetie. I'll be up soon to check
it for you." She really hoped it would be
soon.

The little girl dashed away from the table. It was now Jenny's turn to glare at
Connor.

"Thanks for such a delightful meal!"
she snapped.

"What?"

"I can't believe you didn't do more to
make Angie feel comfortable. You're her
uncle for heaven's sake. At least your father tried to get her to talk, but one look at
your face and she was scared to open her
mouth."

"She's not afraid of me," Connor said.

Jenny rose. "Intimidated is more like it.
When you two gentlemen have finished,
I'll be in my office." She tossed her napkin
on the table and stalked away, as much as
her cane would allow. Tonight she really

wished she was more mobile and could make a dramatic exit.

"Allow me," Connor said beside her, reaching out to open the door from the dining room.

She glanced at him, feeling the warmth from his body envelop hers as she stepped through, almost brushing his arm. He followed her and kept pace as she walked to the office.

Once she was seated behind the desk, Jenny let out her breath. There was nothing she wanted more than to have Connor leave. Maybe he and his father could come to an agreement as to whom would be the best guardian for Angie and both would depart Rocky Point and leave her in peace.

Of course one would take Angie, and she dreaded that. But there was nothing she could do about it.

Brian followed them in hurriedly, looking from one to the other. "I got the name of the lawyer from your sheriff today. He wasn't in this afternoon, but I'll see him in the morning. File custody papers." He stood by the door, his hands nervously playing with the change in his pocket. "Shouldn't take too long for a judge to sign the papers and we'll be on our way back to California."

"No," Connor said.

"And why not?" Brian countered.

"Angie is not going with you."

"I'm her grandfather. Close kin."

"I'm her uncle."

Brian smiled and looked at Jenny as if for support. "Face it, Connor, you aren't the best bet for the child. You're working. Probably gone from home all day and sometimes into the evening. Maybe even travel for business. What do you expect to do with Angie, shunt her off to day care all the time?"

Jenny almost opened her mouth to tell Brian what Connor proposed, but something kept her quiet. She could feel the tension radiating from Connor, anger held in tight leash.

"I'll take care of her," he said.

"I'm retired," Brian continued as if Connor hadn't said a word. "Home all the time. I think a judge would find that more appealing—especially for a little girl who just lost both parents."

The smile Brian gave was sly. For a moment, Jenny wondered if she'd misread the man. He seemed genuinely concerned for his granddaughter. And it would be better for someone to be home all day for Angie—or at least when she got home from school.

"You weren't fit to have kids of your own. You can't raise a little girl now," Connor said tightly.

"Ah, things have changed, Connor my boy. Who do you think a judge will back— a doting grandfather who is home all day, or a carefree bachelor who works and travels?"

"How do you know I'm not married, with a stable home to bring her to?" Connor asked.

"Sheriff Tucker told me all he found out about you. I told him we lost touch. Nice man, that sheriff." Brian rocked back on his heels, his eyes holding a gleam that Jenny found hard to decipher. "We'll see, boy, after I talk with the attorney." He smiled at Jenny. "Thank you for dinner, my dear. I'll be by tomorrow to see Angie." With that, he left.

Connor gazed after him, anger evident.

Jenny cleared her throat and he looked back at her.

"I don't think I need to ask if Andy's parents would consider taking her. If she has a relative willing to have her, I'm sure that's where a judge would think she should go.''

''Not to him,'' Connor said standing. He seemed to loom over her.

''Why not? He's her grandfather. He can be home when she is. He seems to like her.''

''No.'' Connor said, then turned and left.

''Well, that was helpful,'' Jenny murmured. She checked her watch and headed up to spend some time with Angie. Jeffrey was at the front desk. He knew he could call on her anytime if something came up he couldn't handle.

Angie was playing with the new teddy bear when Jenny entered her private suite.

''Are they gone?'' Angie asked.

''Connor and Brian?''

Angie nodded.

''Conner is staying here, remember. Your grandfather is staying at the motel. He'll be back tomorrow.'' Jenny closed the door quietly and went to sit on the sofa. She eased her aching leg up on the small ottoman.

Angie rose and came to sit beside Jenny, leaning against her until Jenny encircled her with her arm.

"I don't want to go anywhere, Jenny. I want to stay here with you. You were mommy's bestest friend, why can't I stay with you? Mommy *loved* you. She and Daddy would love for me to stay here with you. Rocky Point is my home, not California."

"Honey, I'm not related. Usually people live with family. And you have two relatives who both want you to come live with them."

"But I don't know them, and they're guys. I'm a girl. I don't want to go with guys. What if they want me to play football or something."

Jenny smiled, brushing back Angie's hair.

"I doubt they'll expect you to play football unless you want to."

"Why can't I stay with you?"

"It just wouldn't work out." Jenny was so torn. She loved this child of her friend. She wanted only the best for her, but she couldn't provide it. She wasn't sure if Brian or Connor was the right one to care for Angie, but she knew one or the other would obtain custody and take her far away.

For the moment, she cherished the moment, the little girl leaning trustingly against her; the quiet time with just the two of them.

"Let me stay, Jenny. I promise I'll always be good," Angie said softly.

"I wish I could, sweetheart, I truly wish I could."

Two days later Connor strode into the restaurant right at seven the next morning. He looked at the table by the window where Jenny and Angie were eating. When they noticed him, Angie seemed to grow still, wary. He didn't blame her. He'd done a lot of thinking instead of sleeping over the last couple of nights and he had come to a decision.

He walked over and drew a chair from a nearby table to sit with them.

"Good morning," Jenny said gravely.

"Morning."

"Hi, Uncle Connor," Angie said shyly.

"Good morning to you, Angie," he replied. Snagging the coffee carafe, he filled the empty cup from Angie's place and sipped the hot brew. "I want to talk to you," he told Jenny.

"So talk."

"Not here. When we can be alone."

"As soon as Angie leaves for school, I'll have time."

He nodded.

Mrs. Thompson stuck her head around the kitchen door. "Thought I heard another voice. Can I get you breakfast?"

Jenny put down her fork, her appetite gone. What did Connor wish to talk about now? Whisking Angie back to L.A. before his father got to know her? Grilling her in hopes Cathy had said something he could use to show she wanted Connor to raise her daughter?

Cathy had wanted to raise her own daughter. She had never planned to die so young. Jenny slowly sipped her coffee, wishing things had been different.

As soon as Angie finished eating, she jumped up. "I'm going now, Jenny," she said. She came around to give Jenny a hug.

"Bye, Uncle Connor," Angie said.

"Want me to drive you to school again?" Connor asked.

She shook her head. "I'll walk with my friends." She ran from the room.

"We're alone now," Jenny commented, not liking the trepidation that was beginning to build.

"But not free of the possibility of interruptions. We'll talk after breakfast."

"I'm finished now. I'll wait for you in the office."

She couldn't get away fast enough. Connor fascinated her, and worried her. He was only going to be around a little while longer. She could handle the tumultuous feelings that flooded her whenever she saw him.

She had no choice.

He joined her too soon, she thought some time later when he walked in and shut the office door behind him. Instantly he seemed to fill the room, take all the air from her lungs. Jenny took a deep, slow breath, trying to still her jumping nerves.

Crossing to one of the visitor chairs, he sat, leaning back and placing the ankle of one leg on his other knee.

"You know the people in this town. How do you think a judge will rule with Angie," he began.

"If it comes to a custody case, I think any judge would do what he thought was best for her."

"And as you see it that is?"

Jenny toyed with the letter opener, not wanting to take sides, but honesty compelled her to speak her views. "I'd say your lifestyle isn't as suitable for a young child as Brian's appears to be. You work, travel, want to ship her off to some boarding school. Brian's retired and would be home when she was."

"What about a family here in Rocky Point?"

Jenny shrugged. "I can't see a judge ruling in favor of non-family if a relative wanted her. It would be one thing if no one wanted her, but Brian does."

"No."

"No?" She blinked. "He doesn't?"

"He may want what she'll bring, but he can't have her."

"What are you talking about?"

"Angie will inherit a sizable amount from the insurance and will realize more when they liquidate Harrison's assets in the fishing business. Brian wants her money. To get it, he'll take Angie as well."

"That's a pretty harsh view. Maybe he'll put it into a trust for her education like you planned to do," she said.

"Ask him." Connor's tone let Jenny know he didn't believe it for an instant. "But it doesn't matter. He won't get Angie. I haven't seen him for fifteen years, but an investigator turned up a lot of information.''

''And investigator? You had him *investigated?*''

''That first night you told me he was coming, I called L.A. and got someone onto it immediately.''

''And so you turned up enough information to sway a judge?'' Jenny couldn't believe this. ''Did you have me investigated, too?''

''No, should I have?''

She shook her head. ''Did you find out what you wanted about your father?''

Connor frowned. ''Not exactly.''

''What did you find out?''

''That he keeps pretty much to himself. He doesn't work, has some disability payment which keeps him in food and liquor. He lives in a seedy section of town, not where Angie should be.''

''So he can move.''

''With her money, yes he could.''

Connor dropped his leg and leaned forward in his chair. ''I don't want Angie anywhere near him. He was a terrible father and nothing gives me any confidence he's changed. Ask yourself this, Jenny, if he was such a great father, why didn't Cathy keep in touch with him? Why hasn't he visited since she had Angie?''

Jenny frowned. ''You have a point. Cathy never talked about her family. Including you.''

''Never?''

''Rarely. She said once she had a brother in L.A. And that her mother was dead. I thought her father was dead, too.''

''We weren't close.''

That was an understatement, Jenny thought.

''But I'm the better man to raise Angie, than her grandfather. I have a solution.''

''That you shove her off to some boarding school, I suppose.''

''No, that you marry me and we raise Angie together.''

CHAPTER SIX

CONNOR would have found the stunned expression on her face amusing if he didn't want this so strongly. So much for sweeping a woman off her feet.

"Are you crazy?" she asked. "I couldn't marry you. Even if I wanted to, I have no intention of moving to Los Angeles. What's the real story here, marry me, desert us and leave her here? I told you I can't raise Angie."

"I haven't worked out all the details yet, but the plan would work. I know it's asking a lot, but I've seen no sign of a man in your life. It's just for a few years, until she's grown." He was counting on her sense of responsibility, and her obvious caring for his niece.

"She's eight. A *few years* would be ten or twelve minimum."

He nodded.

"You're serious, aren't you?"

"Think about it. I'll move to Rocky

Point. We'll keep her with her friends, in the same school. She already adores you. I'd still have to travel, but I can move most of the administrative functions of the business here. Maybe offer intern programs to some of the students at the college. I haven't worked out all the details. I'm thinking of Angie here.''

''Why can't she go with her grandfather?''

''He'll neglect her like he did Cathy and me. He drinks heavily, Jenny. Once under the influence, he forgets everything else—meals, laundry, the very existence of his children. He's not a mean drunk, just totally dysfunctional.''

Jenny listened to the harsh indictment with growing concern. ''Maybe he's changed,'' she said slowly.

''Maybe he hasn't. According to the investigator's report, he still drinks heavily. He was drinking here last night,'' Connor reminded her. What would it take to get Jenny to agree? There had to be something she wanted enough to trade for a few years of marriage.

''He didn't get drunk last night. Or any other night he's been here.'' But she had smelled liquor on his breath each time he'd showed up. Was Connor right?

"Maybe not here, but ask yourself why is he staying at the motel? Don't you think it would be easier to get to know his grand-daughter if he were staying closer? I think it's because he gets drunk every single night. Is that the kind of life you want to give Angie?"

"Oh, a fake marriage would be so much better? What would you expect her to do if you started dating someone else?"

"Why would I do that?"

Jenny blinked again. Connor felt that stir of amusement. The topic was serious, but he loved watching her, reading almost every thought in her mind by the expres-sions on her face. That comment had caught her short.

"What kind of marriage are you talking about?" she asked warily.

"A real one. Did you think I wanted to expose Angie to someone who treats sacred vows lightly and carries on in defiance of those vows?"

Jenny nodded.

Connor felt a touch of anger. Didn't she know him better than that after the five days he'd been here? Dammit, she should know him better than that instinctively!

"I'm talking real marriage. One no one could challenge," he clarified.

"I don't even like you," Jenny blurted out.

It stung. He knew he wasn't charming like his father. He'd had too many false promises as a child to want to emulate his old man. He was driven to succeed, and often didn't care whose toes he stepped on along the way.

He didn't have to be liked by everyone.

But it hurt that Jenny didn't like him. He liked her. Wanted her.

Stunned with that realization, he rose and walked to the window, gazing unseeingly out on the swirling snow. When had it begun to snow again? Would it keep his father away, or was he planning to drive over this afternoon after school? Planning to continue his charm campaign with Jenny and Angie until both of them were won over? He couldn't let that happen. If nothing else, he owed it to his sister.

"Think about it, okay?" he asked. He wasn't used to being a supplicant. Over the last decade he'd built his business by hard work and sheer determination. And by getting people to do what he wanted. She had to do this. It was the only way he could see to save Angie from his father.

He turned. ''If you want different terms or something, we can negotiate.''

Jenny shook her head. ''This whole thing is crazy. I can't marry you.''

He studied her, seeking a clue to her thoughts. Her eyes blazed. Her cheeks were flushed. The tightening in his gut was not due to her refusal, but something else.

He crossed the room and went around her desk. ''Maybe you're worried about how we'd handle it between us,'' he said.

Her wary gaze never left his. Slowly she shook her head.

''So,'' he leaned closer. ''Maybe we should see…''

Jenny almost bolted from the chair. He was going to kiss her, she knew it. But she couldn't move. Mesmerized, she watched as his head came closer. Just before his lips touched hers, she closed her eyes.

Heaven.

And one of the stupidest things she'd ever done. She had to pull away. She would—in just a moment.

But first, just let her savor the sensations

that zinged through her. Relish the feel of warm lips pressing provocatively against her own. Cherish the sense of femininity that flooded, so long dormant, instantly awakened by desire and passion. Enjoy the tumble of needs that clamored for attention. Delight in the heat that filled every cell.

It had been so long. It had been never. No one had ever kissed her like Connor Wolfe. For an endless moment she was lost in a hazy dream of love and laughter. She and Connor kissing, learning more about each other. Sharing love and life.

Marriage.

Reality crashed down.

She pulled back, breathing hard. "No." Raising her hand, she held it as a shield between them. "I can't marry you."

He stood tall and nodded once. Then he left.

Jenny watched him going, astonished at the yearning that flooded through her. She wished she had stalled him, asked for time to consider his outlandish proposal. Truly given consideration to all the ramifications—and the benefits to Angie. Maybe let him attempt to persuade her with more kisses. Crazy thoughts!

More to the point, she wished she could be the woman Connor Wolfe thought she was.

The snow continued to fall all day. Connor went to pick up Angie from school, determined she wouldn't walk home in what he privately considered blizzard conditions. He was having a hard time accepting Jenny's refusal. Yet was he crazy to volunteer to move to Maine? Who would want to live in winters like this when they could have Tahiti? He was under no illusions about how his life would change if he did marry and move to Rocky Point.

Cilla and Andy came home with Angie. Since skating at the pond was out because of the snowfall, Jenny let the children bake cookies with Mrs. Thompson's help. They soon finished that task, however and were searching for something to do.

With the winter festival fast approaching, the rooms were beginning to fill. Since the weather was bad, the guests were making use of the common area on the main floor and Jenny didn't want the children underfoot.

"Find something to do upstairs," she told Angie. "And quietly." She nodded to the guests. "They are here for peace and quiet, not to hear children making a lot of noise.''

''I know, Jenny. Remember, Mommy used to tell me when we had guests I had to be quiet,'' Angie said solemnly.

Jenny hugged her and then gently pushed Angie toward the stairs. ''Go bug your uncle.''

The children ran gleefully up the stairs. Jenny turned back to the reception desk and went over the room assignments she and Libby had been working on. Before long, she'd need Connor's room. Would he try to find a place at the motel? It was also booked for the festival.

Or maybe he and his father would each return home, leaving Angie in Rocky Point a little longer until the situation could be resolved satisfactorily.

She lost her concentration as she thought of Connor leaving. And remembered his kiss. Should she give some serious thought to his outlandish idea? It would mean so much to Angie to remain in Rocky Point. Maybe she should focus on the child and not on her own feelings in this matter.

''The Sandersons requested a crib, remember?'' Libby said, bringing Jenny back to the task at hand quickly.

"Ask Max to run up to the attic and get one. It'll need to be dusted off, but the mattress was wrapped and the sheets will be clean. Any other special needs?" she asked, knowing she had to pay attention to the details that brought the customers back time after time.

"Just diets, which I've given to Sally already," Libby said, studying some notes she'd made.

Just then Brian entered. Jenny looked up, remembering all Connor had told her about his father. It was hard to believe of such a charming man. Had the man changed since Connor was a child? Or would he be the worst choice for Angie?

"Hi, Brian," Jenny called. She walked from behind the desk. "Angie is upstairs, shall I call her for you?"

"I wanted to speak with you first." He shook his jacket off and brushed the snow from his hair. "It's snowing like crazy outside. How do you stand this weather? I can't wait to get back to the land of sunshine."

"I guess we're used to it here. There is still a spot by the fire we can sit, if you like."

"No, I'd rather talk to you alone first," he said seriously.

It was her day, she sighed. "Come into the office."

Once they were seated, Brian spoke. "I talked to Angie's lawyer this morning. And filled out the papers seeking custody. I can't stay much longer, Jenny. It's too expensive and too cold for me. The sooner I can take Angie to San Diego, the sooner life will return to normal."

"I thought you'd get to know her a little more. Moving to California would be a tremendous change for her." Jenny wanted to protest more strongly, do something to keep Cathy's daughter in Rocky Point. But she had to let her go.

"The motel is booked for the fancy festival you have next week. Unless you have room for me here, I have to leave," he said.

Jenny had no rooms available. She'd been booked for months. Even Connor needed to vacate his room. She'd told him that already. Now she told Brian.

"So we'll both be out of your hair soon," he said.

"Jenny, Jenny, you were famous!" Angie burst into the office, wearing a sparkling tiara, waving two magazines. Cilla followed, carrying two shimmering outfits, with Andy coming up behind with a flat wooden box. Their faces beamed with excitement.

"Look, you were in a *magazine!*" Angie plopped one of the familiar sports journals down on Jenny's desk, her face beaming. "They have your picture and everything."

A younger Jenny looked up from the color photo, her eyes sparkling, her smile dazzling. Karl close by.

"Can we wear these when we go skating?" Cilla asked, holding up one of the fancy leotards Jenny remembered wearing at a World Cup event.

"Jennifer Gordon, darling of the Olympics trials, a shoo-in for winning the gold. What happened?" Connor stood in the doorway, surveying the jumping children, the speculative look on his father's face, and the shock on Jenny's.

Emotions roiled through her, sparking instant action. Without thought, she rose and came around the desk to snatch the magazine Angie still held. "Where did you get these? They aren't yours!" Reaching out, she yanked the costumes Cilla was waving around. "How dare you go into my private things! Give me those and get out of my office!" She pulled the tiara from

Angie's hair, ignoring the stricken expression on the little girl's face.

Dumping them on the desk, she reached for the box of medals Andy held. He relinquished them without protest, a stricken look in his eyes.

"All of you, get out!" Slowly she turned and leaned against the desk, stunned at the emotions that swept through her like a tidal wave. She needed the support of the desk. Given the sharp pain in her hip, it was all she could do to remain upright. She tried to breathe through the constriction in her throat. She hadn't seen these things in years. How dare those children invade her privacy! A million thoughts jumbled in her mind as she stared at the signs of past glories. Over all, the pain of loss threatened to consume her.

She heard the children creep out.

Brian rose and left.

The door shut.

She closed her eyes, the humiliation and regret almost overwhelming. Resting against her hands, she tried to breathe. She'd have to sit down soon, her leg was giving her fits. But first she needed to find some control.

"I thought you looked familiar,"

Connor said. "I must have seen you a hundred times on ESPN."

Jenny opened her eyes and turned to glare at him. He was leaning casually against the door, arms crossed over his chest.

"Get out," she said.

"Make me," he taunted.

"I don't want you here."

"I don't especially want to be here, but we still have unfinished business."

"No, we don't."

He nodded to the things piled on the desk.

"They are just children. They were happy to find out some terrific news about someone they all look up to. You were too hard on them."

She swallowed. She didn't need Connor to tell her that. But seeing it all again had been unexpected and she'd reacted without thinking.

"Well, if nothing else, that should point out to you how unsuited I'd be as a stepmother," she said, unwilling to admit to Connor how wrong she'd been. She'd have to apologize to Angie and Cilla and Andy, however. As soon as she got her emotions under control.

He shrugged, still staying by the door as if to give her space. "You're only human. Obviously it upset you a lot."

"Obviously," she repeated dryly. Her heart rate was back under control, her breathing almost normal. The anger and grief already fading.

"So what's the story? You were destined for greatness, why get upset because Angie just found out?"

"It was a bad time."

"Being famous?"

"Being on the eve of the Olympics and then—" She turned away. She didn't want talk about it. Limping to her chair, she sat down gratefully, rubbing her hip, wishing her pain medicine was close at hand. She rarely took any, fighting the pain in other ways, but today she could use it.

"And then? Is that when you had your accident?" he asked.

She hesitated, then nodded. It was not as if it were a secret. A quick trip to the library to read old newspapers would give most of the story.

Or he could talk to anyone in town. They'd be sure to tell him how she'd let them all down—her father, Karl, the entire town of Rocky Point, Maine, by her foolishness, her selfishness.

"Tough break."

"Literally," she said with a mirthless laugh.

"And that's tied to your reason for not marrying me to take care of Angie, isn't it?" he said astutely.

She gazed out the window a moment, seeing things as they'd been at that time. "I let them all down. I can't be depended upon. What if Angie needed me and I let her down?" she said slowly, regretfully. She'd change it if she could, she would have all those years ago, if only she'd been given the chance.

"What are you talking about?"

"My father—he trained me toward the Olympics all my life. Then through an act of defiance, I ruined everything. I let him down. It had all been for nought. The years of sacrifice. The endless hours of practice. He...he died while I was still in the hospital."

Connor hadn't moved. Didn't offer flowery words of sentiment. He just watched her. Jenny flicked her gaze his way, as if waiting for his condemnation.

"I also let down my partner. Karl and I

had trained together for years. When we made the cut for the Olympics, we were thrilled to death.'' God, she could still remember the excitement, the dazzling promise of the future. Those had been heady days.

''So what was this act of defiance?'' Connor asked.

Slowly the old memories surfaced. ''We were in Boston. The next morning we were due to depart—on our way to Olympic Village. A friend of mine lived in town and called me to go out with her for a celebratory night on the town. I was supposed to be asleep in my room, getting rest before our trip. Instead, I snuck out to go with Cassie. A drunk driver came out of nowhere and slammed into her car. She's in a wheelchair to this day. The doctors didn't know at first if I'd ever walk again. I ruined so many lives all for a night of stolen fun.''

''As I said, tough break. But I don't see how you ruined anything. You were injured in the crash.'' Connor's voice sounded calm, rational.

''If I hadn't snuck out, Cassie would have stayed home. No one would have been hurt. Karl and I would have had our shot at the gold. My dad...my dad would still be alive.''

''And you would not have been injured.''

She shrugged her shoulders dismissingly. ''It's not as bad as Cassie. At least I can walk.''

''What happened to the drunk driver?''

''He was killed instantly. He left a wife and two small children. What a waste.''

''I still don't see the connection with my offer. Don't you want to help Angie?''

''Dammit, Connor, aren't you listening? My father told me how unreliable I was. How so many people had been depending on me and I let them all down. He railed at how stupid and selfish and self-centered I had been. Karl ranted and raved about my actions. Because of what happened, he lost his shot at the gold. It's hard to compete in pairs skating when your partner is in a hospital bed. By the next Olympics, it was too late for him. The people from town who came to see me talked about how disappointed everyone was that I didn't skate for the gold. I let everyone down. It's something I have to live with. I dare not let anyone depend on me again.''

''Bull!''

"What?"

"How old were you?"

"Nineteen. What does that have to do with anything?"

"A nineteen-year-old kid does not have the responsibility to carry the world on her shoulders—or even the hopes and aspirations of a small town in Maine. You went out for some fun. If nothing had happened, you'd have snuck back in, gotten a few hours less sleep than normal and gone off to skate, right?"

"I guess."

"Bad luck changed things, but you didn't do anything wrong. You didn't let anyone down."

"I did," she whispered. "My dad…Connor, he was yelling at me when he had a heart attack and died—right there in my hospital room. He just collapsed and sank down to the floor. They couldn't save him."

"He had no business yelling at you when you were in the hospital. Jenny, you did nothing wrong."

"I did—"

He shook his head and pushed away from the door, crossing the room until he leaned on the desk with his hands, putting his face close to hers. "No, you did what any nineteen-year-old might have done, went in search of some fun. I know how grueling training for sporting events can be. Everyone needs to let loose once in a while."

"Karl said—"

"I don't care what he said, he was speaking from frustration and disappointment. It was unfortunate the accident happened at all, and especially on the eve of the Olympics, but that's life. Deal with it. But don't let it color the rest of your existence. Move on."

She blinked at him. "I did. I have this Inn."

"Which shows how dependable and reliable you can be."

"What?"

"How long have you had it?"

"Almost since I got out of rehab. I used the money from the driver's insurance company to start it up."

"You employee how many people? Seven that I've counted."

She nodded. "Full-time. I hire college kids to fill in when it gets crowded—like next week when the February Festival is on or during the summer."

"So at least seven other people know they can depend upon you for their livelihoods. Who else depends on you? I know Angie does. She trusts you implicitly. I bet she got that from her mother."

"It doesn't matter."

"How would you let Angie down?"

"Didn't this scene just show you?"

"You were caught by surprise. Now you'll apologize, she'll forgive you and we go on. But if she were sick in the night, you would go to her. If she has a play at school, you'd attend. If she needs new clothes, you'd provide them. I can't see how in the world you'd ever let her down. She needs you. I need you. Marry me, Jenny. For Angie's sake. For the ten years it takes until Angie turns eighteen. Help me out. I trust you, I know we can depend upon you."

It was tantalizing. To know she'd be with Angie while she was growing up. To make sure her best friend's daughter had all the love and devotion she could give.

The memory of Connor's kiss flashed into mind. He'd said it would be a real marriage. That would mean more kisses, making love.

Having children?

No, not if it was a temporary marriage of convenience. Not if they were planning to divorce once Angie was grown. She would not have a child with that hanging over her head.

"Say yes, Jenny," he urged.

She studied the intensity in his dark eyes, the rigid control he held as if his sheer will-power would entice her to give him the answer he wanted. He was a man who knew what he wanted, and went after it all the way. He unsettled her. And had her yearning for something she didn't know if she could ever have.

Could it work?

Only time would tell. Was she brave enough to chance it?

CHAPTER SEVEN

CONNOR watched the expressions chase across Jenny's face. He had to tell her never to play poker, she'd give away every thought. He knew the turmoil was taking its toll, but hoped her love for his niece would swing the balance in his favor.

He wanted her. And he'd excelled in getting what he wanted over the last few years. The kiss had been a surprise. Or rather, his reaction to her soft lips, the sweet taste of her, had been the surprise. He couldn't remember ever feeling so strongly for a woman he hardly knew. Or any other woman, for that matter.

But this wasn't about him. It was about his past, his sister and the niece he'd protect at all costs from his father.

"Jenny, Angie needs you. You've seen me and my father. He got all the charm, I got none. I don't try to soft soap things, dance around things. I go for the jugular. I shoot straight and don't lie. That's the lesson I learned from my parents." He hoped the bitterness wouldn't notch up another mark against him. He knew she didn't like him very much, but he'd never been able to be anyone but who he was.

"If we go before a judge in this town, who do you think he'll give custody to— me or my father?" he asked.

"Brian," was her reluctant response.

"I've told you about him. Do you want Angie to be exposed to that? Surely Cathy's never talking about our family told you something."

"I didn't speak much of my father. We just let the past stay behind."

"For a similar reason—regrets. She didn't see him a lot even as a child." He stood and ran his hand through his hair in frustration. He didn't think he was getting through to her and time was running out.

"She mentioned you once, years ago," Jenny said. "She had always hoped you two would draw closer."

Connor looked at her, hope blossoming. "I wish we had, too. I want to make it up to her by taking Angie. The child would be better off with me. And with you."

She stared at him so long he grew impatient. But he let none of his feelings show. He'd waited longer for other deals, but none had felt as important as this one.

"Okay, Connor, I'll marry you for Angie's sake," she said at last.

He felt a wave of relief surge through him, then triumph. She would be his!

"As soon as possible, I'd suggest," Jenny added, standing and reaching for her cane. "Your father has already filed custody papers."

"What?"

"He told me just before the children came in." Her eyes rested sadly on the still-opened magazine.

Connor wanted to reach out and touch her. Offer comfort for the sadness so evident. The thought surprised him. He wasn't into touchy-feely stuff. Not that she'd find much comfort from him. She shied away anytime he came near.

Not every time. The memory of their kiss mocked.

When she passed the desk, heading for the door, he stopped her.

"As soon as we can do it," he said softly, leaning over to kiss her again. She was going to be his wife. He could hardly wait.

Her lips trembled slightly when his

pressed against them. Then he felt a slight sigh as she gave herself up to the pleasure of the kiss. Reaching out, he pulled her into his embrace, hoping for a modicum of restraint lest he overwhelm her with the unexpected need that exploded.

His tongue sought entrance, found it. Shyly she responded when his tongue danced with hers. The exploration of the kiss changed, deepened and drove the desire already present to new heights.

Connor realized he could kiss her forever. Only kissing wouldn't be enough. He wanted to touch her, learn the texture of her skin, absorb the sweet scent of her body. Make her his.

The knock on the door ended the kiss before Connor was ready. He made sure she was steady on her feet before crossing the short distance and flinging the door wide.

Libby stood there, her expression worried. "The children tore out of here so unexpectedly, I wanted to make sure things were all right. I think Angie was crying."

"I shouted at them," Jenny said, moving toward the door. "I shouldn't have. I'll go up to them now and apologize."

"Can I do anything?" the older woman

asked, her glance flicking to Connor, then back to Jenny.

"No, but thanks, Libby. I appreciate the offer."

"Jenny and I will be getting married," Connor said as he followed Jenny from the office.

"Married? Congratulations," Libby said, looking stunned.

Jenny frowned at Connor. "I wanted to tell Angie first," she said.

He shrugged. The sooner everyone knew she'd agreed to marry him, the harder it would be for her to change her mind. He wondered how soon they could get married in Maine. Maybe they should just fly to Las Vegas today and—

"Are you coming with me?" Jenny asked, already heading for the stairs, leaning heavily on her cane.

"Absolutely." He stepped forward and swept her up in his arms again. Stepping to the stairs he began to climb.

"Put me down, I can manage," she protested, but one arm clung around his neck.

"So can I." She didn't weigh that much. Was she in constant pain, or only on certain occasions? Why did she have a business with stairs if walking was such a chore?

There was a lot about this woman he needed to know.

When they reached the second floor, Jenny insisted on being put down. She walked down the hall as if heading for his room. Where was she going? Opposite his door, she stopped before a door marked Private and seemed to gather herself. She knocked briefly and opened it, stepping inside. Connor followed and stopped. Obviously a suite, it was Jenny's private quarters. The sitting room was cozy, with a chintz-covered Early American sofa, and comfortable chairs flanking the rough-hewn coffee table. Angie's skates were on the floor, her jacket flung on a chair.

The three children sat on the sofa, staring at Jenny with trepidation.

She slowly walked to the coffee table and lowered herself to sit on it. Looking at each child gravely, she said, "I apologize for yelling at you. I'm very sorry. It was wrong of me and I won't do it again. You caught me by surprise and I lost my temper. Please forgive me."

"Oh, Jenny, we're sorry we went into your things!" Angie launched herself into Jenny's arms. The way they tightened around the child showed Connor all he needed to know about Jenny's care of his niece.

Their marriage wouldn't be in name only. He'd made that clear. She hadn't voiced a protest to the original terms. Should he have mentioned it again?

Cilla and Andy stood on either side, patting Jenny's shoulder and offering apologies of their own.

Connor felt odd watching the scene. There was a bond among them all that he'd never felt. This would blow over and they'd resume their easy relationship. Jenny would still be on good terms with the children.

He didn't know how to talk to Angie or her friends. Hell, he didn't even know how to talk to Jenny. He was no good at the family thing. His relationship with his father and his sister proved that. What made him think he would do differently with his niece?

Jenny did. He watched her smile at the children and offer a treat in the kitchen. How quickly some situations were resolved.

"Are you coming with us, Uncle Connor?" Angie said as she saw him blocking the door. "Mrs. Thompson makes the best sundaes in the world."

"It's snowing outside. I like my ice cream when it's hot out," he said. Glancing at Jenny, he looked back at Angie.

"Wait a minute before you go. I want you to know something, and your friends can hear it, too."

"Connor." Jenny rose.

He held out his hand to her, watching to see what she'd do. Was she having second thoughts already?

She raised her chin and struck out across the small distance that separated them. Taking his hand, she let him pull her close.

"Jenny and I are going to get married and have you live with us, Angie," he said.

"Wow," Angie said, looking at Jenny with a bright smile. "Does that mean I get to call you Aunt Jenny?"

"If you like."

"Yes!" The little girl jumped up and down and then hugged her friends. "Now I don't have to go to California with Grandpa Brian. I get to stay here!"

Connor's grip tightened on Jenny's hand when she almost spoke.

"We'll discuss things later, you better

head for that hot fudge sundae Jenny promised you,'' Connor said.

The children ran down the hall, their cheerful voices ringing.

''Great, probably disturbing every guest we have,'' Jenny said wryly.

''It's too early to disturb anyone.''

Jenny looked at him. ''Are you sure you can move here?''

''You can't move to California and run the Inn.''

''So how will this marriage work?'' she asked.

''However we set it up to work.'' He leaned over and kissed her again.

After Angie was in bed, Jenny went to soak in a hot bath. Her hip and leg had ached all day, ever since her abrupt end-run around the desk. The hot water soothed her. Bubbles floated and popped softly around her. She loved bubble baths. It was the best part of evenings—after Angie was asleep. The only down side was the amount of time she had to think.

And all thoughts centered on her agreement to marry Connor Wolfe and make a home for Angie.

Heat swept through her. Maybe all

thoughts weren't of their outlandish agreement. His kiss sparked feelings in her she didn't know she was capable of. She'd held off the men she'd dated over the years since Karl. Once they'd talked of marriage—and skating. That was so long ago.

Connor was nothing like the men she normally dated. Maybe that was why the feelings he evoked were as intense as he was. He didn't give her time to think—only feel and react. How would marriage to him be?

A real honest-to-goodness marriage with a shared bed, meals together and a united front for Angie. The hot bath seemed suddenly cool in comparison to her body temperature.

Brian had not offered congratulations. He'd glared at Connor when her future husband had coolly informed him of their plans, assuring Connor that wasn't the end of the matter.

She'd heard Connor taunt him about wanting Angie's money, and Brian had all but admitted it, saying he'd need it to raise the child properly. Would she have believed him had Connor not told her of his childhood? Or of the detective's report?

Drying off a little later, she donned her

flannel nightie and robe. Even though the old Inn was as weather tight as she could get it, she felt the cold. Maybe she should consider Connor's suggestion of moving to California. At least she'd be warm.

But what of Angie and her school and friends? Of her love for ice skating? She didn't want to take the child from all she knew and loved.

She'd had a lot to think about in the tub, especially Connor's assessment that she had done nothing wrong when she'd been nineteen. It was a novel concept, one Jenny was having a hard time accepting, no matter how much she longed to do just that!

When she went out into the sitting room, Jenny was startled to see Connor sitting on her sofa, Angie leaning up against him, sound asleep. The sports magazines the children had discovered earlier spread around them. He was reading one of the articles. He glanced up when she came in and stopped as his gaze drifted from the top of her head to her toes peeping beneath her nightie.

''I thought Angie was in bed,'' she said softly.

''I came to see you, she answered the door and didn't want to go back to bed. She misses her mother and father,'' he said softly.

Jenny nodded, crossing over to sit on the edge of the coffee table, reaching out to brush a strand of hair off the child's face. ''She cries herself to sleep a lot. I don't know what to do about it.''

''Probably not much you can do. She needs a chance to grieve, let her. I'll take her in to bed.''

Jenny looked at the magazines, sighing softly. ''Why are these here?''

''She wanted me to read them to her. She's so excited to learn you were such a famous skater. Maybe you can give her pointers. You don't really mind her knowing about it, do you?''

''I guess not. It's…'' It was hard to explain. She felt that teenager had been totally different from the woman she was today—as if it all had happened to someone else. It seemed strange to see her young face staring back up at her from the photographs.

''Feeling better?'' he asked, picking up the little girl and heading for her bedroom. Angie didn't waken, but instinctively snuggled against her uncle.

''Yes. Why did you come by?''

His smile was mocking. "Didn't you think we needed some time together? We're getting married soon. Three days from tomorrow." With that he crossed into Angie's bedroom to put her to bed.

Jenny rose and stacked the magazines face down on the table. She sat on one of the chairs and gently rubbed her aching leg.

She knew they had to move swiftly, to present the judge with a fait accompli before Brian came up with a counter move. But it felt like they were rushing headlong into disaster.

"So you wanted to make plans?" she said when he returned. Gingerly, she tucked her bare feet beneath the chair. Jenny was not as comfortable around Connor as she needed to be to pull this marriage off. His presence unsettled her.

"Plans can be good." He sprawled back on the sofa studying her. His dark pants and shirt looked out of place against the light-colored furniture. He radiated assurance, confidence and masculine sex appeal!

As he continued to study her, Jenny grew restless, conscious she had nothing on beneath her robe but her nightie.

"So," she had to break the silence, it

was driving her crazy. "We get married on Friday."

He nodded. "Didn't Libby tell me yesterday you needed my room this weekend?"

Jenny nodded. "The festival will be starting and we've been booked for months."

"So I move in here."

She caught her breath. They'd be sharing a room—a bed. She wished she had longer to get used to the idea. To get used to *him!*

"There's not a lot of room."

"I don't take up much space," he said, amusement in his eyes.

It didn't seem like it to her, whenever he was in a room he seemed to fill it to the brim. "What about your business in L.A.?"

"I'll be returning soon. Once things are squared away here."

She was surprised at the disappointment she felt when she heard that. Make up your mind, she silently chided herself. Either you want him here or not!

"I'll open a satellite office here in Rocky Point. It'll only be for a few years. The bulk of the operation will remain in L.A. I need the West Coast contacts and access to my current customers and to shipping. I'll have to travel more than I've been doing. But this can be home," he explained.

"Did you want us to move there?"

"Do you want to? Your Inn is here. Angie's friends are here." For a moment he grew quiet. "I would have given a lot for the stability she has in her life. I don't want to be the one to shake that."

Jenny nodded. Angie did have continuity, but did she really have stability?

"I've lived here all my life. But in the depth of winter, I'd love to be on a hot beach somewhere," she confessed.

"There are plenty of those in Southern California."

"I know. But you're right, we are doing this for Angie, and her life right now is here. She adores skating. I imagine there isn't much ice in L.A."

"I'm sure there are rinks. Do you think she's good enough to compete?"

Jenny shook her head. "Don't even go there. It's not an easy life and she's had enough hardships without taking that on."

"So you don't miss skating?"

"I do sometimes, but for the joy of skating, not for the hard work and endless hours of practice, striving always for perfection, for a more challenging spin, or jump, or manoeuver. It was hard work. My dad was after me constantly, practice before school, after school, weekends. I don't miss that.''

"How long did you do it?''

"From the time I was six until the accident when I was nineteen.''

"Lucky you lived here.''

She shrugged. "Maybe if we hadn't, I would have had a more normal childhood,'' she said slowly. "That's what I want for Angie.'' Jenny met his gaze, holding his with the fervor of her emotions. "I really want that for Angie. Stability, love, security, and a chance to be a child.''

"And for yourself, what do you want from this marriage?'' Connor asked.

"To feel we aren't making the world's greatest mistake, I guess,'' she said softly.

"Tomorrow we'll go for the license and stop by to see the attorney. Maybe look at a couple of houses.''

"Houses?''

"You didn't think we would live here, did you?''

Jenny blinked. "Yes, I guess I did.''

"You wanted a normal life for Angie. The three of us cramped into this suite isn't normal. Beside, if you live off premises, you can rent out this suite.''

''I hadn't thought about moving.''

''No matter where we live in Rocky Point, it won't be as if you'll have a long commute,'' he responded dryly.

''Is your father planning to attend the ceremony?''

''I hope not.''

''I think he and Angie should both be there,'' she said.

''Maybe Angie, though she'd have to miss school. But not my father.'' Connor's tone was final.

But it didn't deter Jenny. ''He is her grandfather. I thought we were showing a united front.''

He narrowed his eyes slightly. ''We are, he has nothing to do with this.''

''It'll be easier all around. And show we are doing the best for Angie.''

''Are you always argumentative?'' he asked.

''I'm not arguing, just pointing out some facts. We'll show the world we are a family.''

''Complete with doting grandfather. He wouldn't dare show his true colors in case there is still a chance he could get Angie.''

"There isn't a chance he could, is there?" she asked, suddenly worried.

"You know the judges here, what do you think?"

"I don't know any judges, but I think anyone would let her stay here with us—especially when you are not asking for any money from the estate."

She shifted slightly, trying to get comfortable. What she really wanted was to go right to bed. Maybe lying down would ease the ache. If she could just get a good night's sleep, she'd be fine in the morning.

"Leg bothering you?" he asked.

"Hip, really. I just need to get to bed."

"Are you in pain all the time?"

"No. Just if I move," she tried to lighten the mood with a joke, but it fell flat. Connor wasn't the joking type.

"Get to bed, Jenny. Time enough for plans in the future."

She couldn't imagine what all the future held for them. She only hoped it would prove worthwhile for Angie.

CHAPTER EIGHT

Connor paused in the doorway to the dining room the next morning. Angie and Jenny were seated at a table for four. He was struck by the bond that apparently already existed between them. He knew his niece missed her parents, last night had clearly shown that, but she also seemed content to be taken care of by Jenny. It reaffirmed his decision as nothing else could have.

"Did you two sleep well?" he asked Jenny, sitting opposite her a moment later.

Angie nodded energetically. "I slept fine, did you take me to my bed, Uncle Connor?"

"I did, and you weigh a ton!"

She giggled.

He looked at Jenny, raising an eyebrow.

"I slept fine."

"Is there something more that can be done to ease that pain?"

"Not that Doctor Rankin has mentioned."

"When was the last time you asked?"

Angie studied Connor. "Are you mad at Jenny?"

"No."

"You look mad."

He glanced at Jenny.

She smiled. "You do, a bit."

Connor bared his teeth in a mock grin. "This better?"

Angie giggled again. Jenny almost did. She would never have expected that from the man.

"Marginally," she replied, knowing her eyes must reflect her amusement.

"We'll head for town when we take Angie to school."

"Can I be a flower girl in the wedding?"

"Of course," Jenny said at the same time Connor shook his head. "It won't be that kind of wedding."

They looked at each other.

"I thought the justice of the peace," he said.

"I thought Reverend Tinsdale in the chapel at the college."

Angie looked back and forth between

them until Mrs. Thompson entered carrying a tray with hot biscuits, coffee and milk.

"Can I?" she asked again.

"We'll discuss it after school today," Jenny said. If she and Connor were to present a united front, they should start with the very first issue of this unusual marriage—the ceremony.

Two hours later, Jenny and Connor left the courthouse, marriage license in hand. In three days they could get married.

"Time to discuss the wedding," she said.

"I think the justice of the peace is all we need. You don't have family here to give you away, no family on my part."

"What about your father."

"I don't plan for him to show up."

For a moment Jenny wanted to argue about his father and about the ceremony. But he was right. Her dad wasn't here to see her get married. Her best friend had been Cathy. She had other friends, but none as close. And with the temporary nature of the marriage, maybe it would be best to keep it as business-like as possible.

But secretly she yearned for a white dress, attendants and lots of flowers. And her father to give her away.

"Okay, Friday at eleven thirty with a judge. Could we have a wedding lunch at least? You'll be surprised at how people will rally round in a small town. Libby, Sally, the kids who work for me on the front desk. They'll all want to wish us well."

He looked at her and Jenny could almost see the argument forming as he considered her idea. But he surprised her, shrugging. "Do whatever you wish, just don't expect me to help."

"I'll do better on my own. I have a lot to do with the February Festival coming up. You run along, Connor. I'll see you back at the Inn later."

He watched her start across the street, cane in hand. He felt completely dismissed. It was not something he was used to. Nor was the feelings of protection that rose every time he was around Jenny Gordon. He wanted to sweep her up and carry her so her leg wouldn't ache. Find a doctor who would provide a cure. Erase the bad memories of the past and make new ones that would bring a smile to her face.

Instead, he was almost coercing her into a marriage she didn't want, that he didn't want. All to keep Angie from his father's clutches.

"How will you get back to the Inn?" he called.

She turned and waved, reaching the opposite sidewalk safely. "I'll get a lift."

His cell phone rang just as he entered the florist shop. "Wolfe," he said.

"Boss, we've got a major problem. I think you need to deal with it," Stephanie began.

An hour later Connor was on his way to L.A. He'd left a note at the front desk for Jenny, packed his bag and headed for the nearest airport. Stephanie had already booked his flight and he'd be in Los Angeles before dark, California time.

When he'd told Jenny he wouldn't be any help, he hadn't meant he'd leave entirely. But the situation at the office was serious and he needed to get it resolved before it escalated out of hand.

He could also use a day in Los Angeles to get the ball rolling for relocating many of the major company positions to Rocky Point. He wondered how he'd broach the subject to Stephanie.

Once on the highway, he reviewed his plans. He couldn't believe he was leaving a major West Coast city for a dinky little town in eastern Maine. How far apart could the two places be!

It did no good reminding himself it was temporary. Ten years was a long temporary assignment. As far as he was concerned, he was getting a ready-made family. Not that he knew much about family life. The examples he'd had growing up were not ones he wanted to repeat. But he could learn. The most important thing was to keep Angie happy.

Or, maybe it was equally important to bring some happiness into Jenny's life. She'd gotten a raw deal and didn't seem to feel she deserved more. He planned to change that as well.

He almost laughed in derision. Connor Wolfe, White Knight. He was a selfish bastard and knew it. Jenny probably thought so as well. But he'd do the best he could for the years they were married. He'd learned long ago to depend only on himself. Nothing would change with a few words in a ceremony.

When Jenny returned home, it was late afternoon. She was so tired and achy all she wanted was to take some pain pills and lie down. She missed Cathy all the time, but especially now with the February Festival coming on. Cathy had been her right-hand man and had almost done the work of two. Jenny missed her business acumen right now more than ever.

One of the college kids was at the front desk.

"Where's Libby?" she asked Daniel.

"Had a bad tooth. The dentist could squeeze her in this afternoon, so she called me in. I can work my normal evening shift as well, no problem."

"Thanks, Daniel, that's a help. I'm going up to lie down. Would you please make sure Angie comes in before dark?" Angie was already home from school, outside skating with her friends.

"Will do."

Jenny slowly climbed the stairs, wondering where Connor was. Working in his room, most likely. He spent a lot of time on his computer and the phone. Tomorrow she could do more by phone and save wear and tear on her leg.

Lying down she gratefully closed her eyes, it was bliss to be off her feet. She ran through all the things she had to do as she drifted off to sleep.

*   *   *

"Jenny?" Angie shook her shoulder again. "It's dinner time and I'm starved. Are you sick?"

Jenny woke and looked sleepily at the little girl. "No, honey, I'm just resting. I didn't mean to sleep so long."

"Where's Uncle Connor?"

"I don't know. If he's not downstairs, he's probably in his room working."

"No, I knocked. It's empty."

"Out somewhere then."

"He took his suitcase."

Jenny sat up, the last vestiges of sleep vanishing. "What?"

"His room is empty. He took his clothes and his suitcase."

Quickly she scanned her own room. Had he already moved in? She rose and opened the closet door. Only her things. Maybe he was planning to move in later and had packed in preparation.

Or maybe he was gone.

Jenny felt sick. He couldn't have gone. They were getting married in three days.

He'd never wanted to get married. Had seeing the license proved how close reality of marriage was and he bolted?

No, she wouldn't believe that. It had been his idea. Besides, she'd bet the Inn he was not the type to bolt if things got too tough. He'd mow down the opposition, more likely.

"Let's go down to dinner. I bet he shows up in time to eat," Jenny said, hoping she sounded more confident than she felt. Surely Connor would join them for the meal.

Brian rose from one of the chairs near the fireplace when they descended.

"Angie, come give grandpa a hug," he boomed. Several guests turned and smiled.

Angie went over willingly enough and gave him a perfunctory hug. "Where's Uncle Connor?"

Brian looked at Jenny. "Not here?"

"Apparently not. You haven't seen him?"

"I'm the last person he wants to see," he told them both. Smiling at Angie, he continued, "I didn't see you yesterday young lady and I wanted to see you again before I go back to California."

"Join us for dinner, Brian," Jenny said, curious about the man Connor held in such dislike. So far except for the desire for Angie's money, he'd seemed the perfect grandfather. Maybe if she got to know him better, she could see what Connor saw. Or maybe Brian had changed over the years. Maybe things weren't just as Connor remembered them.

"Delighted dear lady. Lead on."

As the meal progressed, Jenny learned that she was not cut out to be an investigator. As far as she could tell, Brian was just what he appeared to be—a father still grieving the loss of a daughter, and trying to get to know his granddaughter.

Jenny continued to wonder where Connor was. When they'd finished eating, Angie and Brian went to watch some television in the lounge while she went to her office. In passing the front desk she asked if anyone had called for her. Daniel shook his head.

By bedtime, Jenny was fearful Connor had just left. Had he changed his mind about marriage after all? Had it only been a ploy to make sure his father didn't get custody of Angie? Perhaps he had never planned to go through with the ceremony, expecting Brian to give up and leave before Friday. But then why go as far as he had with the charade if he didn't plan to follow through?

The next morning once Angie was off to school, Jenny called the attorney's office to get Connor's phone number in L.A. The secretary refused to divulge the information, but did agree to call there to see if anyone knew where Connor was and ask them to call Jenny directly.

Ten minutes later Connor called.

"Where are you?" Jenny asked, anger flaring. How dare he just up and leave!

"In L.A. Is something wrong?"

"You tell me. One minute we're getting a marriage license, the next, you've disappeared."

"I said I'd be back before the ceremony."

"To whom did you say that? There was no message, no phone call, nothing. How am I supposed to know where you take off to?" She was overreacting. But she couldn't seem to keep the frustration from her voice.

"I left word with Libby. An emergency came up. I'll handle it and be back there by Friday morning. Eleven thirty, right?"

"Libby went home early yesterday with a toothache," she said slowly. Maybe she had forgotten to give Jenny the message.

"Jenny, I would not disappear without leaving word."

She swallowed, relieved to hear his

voice, shaken to know how much she had feared he'd done just that.

"You could have called yesterday," he said.

She heard voices in the background, heard Connor tell them to wait another minute. He had some emergency, and she was tying him up on the phone.

"I didn't have your number. I never got it. I'll see you Friday, then."

"You can count on it, Jenny." The line went dead.

It would be so nice to count on Connor, she thought wistfully when she hung up. Did he hope he could count on her?

The angry words of her father echoed in her mind. "I miss you, dad," she said softly, feeling the weight of the past again. If only she could relive that night, she'd do things so differently.

Was she doing the right thing taking Angie on? Jenny silently vowed to Cathy that she'd do her best by her daughter. She wouldn't let Angie forget her mother as she had hers. She wouldn't force Angie into a life with a single focus and let her miss the normal rites of passage for children. And she would always love her best friend's daughter.

And her best friend's brother?

The thought crept insidiously in.

Jenny shook her head. She was not falling in love with Connor. The very idea was ludicrous. Ridiculous. Impossible.

Friday morning, Angie was more excited about the wedding than Jenny. As the time approached, she had butterflies in her stomach and constantly questioned if she was doing the right thing.

Angie danced around the room, wearing a pretty Sunday dress, and delighted to be allowed to skip school for the event.

"I get to call you Auntie Jenny after the ceremony, right? You'll be my aunt and Uncle Connor is my uncle."

"Right." Oh God, and Connor would be returning to the Inn after the ceremony— her husband. She looked around her bedroom, cleaned and tidy beyond usual. She'd moved some clothes to allow him room in the closet, but it felt surreal. She couldn't really expect to share—

"I told Cilla I'd tell her everything. Are we ready to go yet?" Angie asked.

"In a minute." She checked herself in the mirror. The suit was new, a pale blue. The color was her favorite. If she couldn't be a bride in a white dress walking in with her father, she at least wanted her favorite color.

"I have a surprise," Angie said, her eyes dancing in excitement.

For a moment Jenny's heart was struck by the joy in the child's eyes. Her mother should be here to see her. For the first time since the fire, Angie looked completely happy. Jenny knew she would never get over losing her parents, but at least Jenny felt she was doing her best to keep Angie safe and happy. She knew this marriage was the right thing.

"I'm ready, I just need my cane."

"I'll get it!" Angie dashed into her room and came out a moment later. The cane had been festively decorated with white ribbon and bows. "I did the decorating myself. Libby helped a little, but mostly it was me," she said proudly.

Jenny felt a tug in her heart. She did so love this child. "Thank you, Angie. It's beautiful!"

They set out together, walking down the stairs. At the bottom, her staff gathered. Libby was driving them to the ceremony, but Jenny had invited them all to lunch upon their return. She had wanted to hire a different cook for the event so Sally could enjoy it, but the woman insisted she was the only one to do them justice.

Everyone cheered. Jenny was touched.

"Ready?" Libby asked.

"Does she have something old?" Sally asked.

Jenny shook her head.

"Here, my mother's handkerchief. I carried it myself. It'll bring you good luck."

"Something new?" Margie called out.

"My suit, and it's blue. And I'm borrowing Sally's handkerchief, so that's the borrowing bit."

Libby stepped forward and placed a small hat with veil on her head. "That completes it, I think."

Jenny was starting to feel funny about all the fuss. It was almost a business arrangement after all. Not that anyone could know that. She and Connor had agreed that to the world it would appear real. Actually, he planned to make it real. Her heart fluttered again at the thought.

Max stepped out from around Daniel and presented Jenny with a huge bouquet of flowers, and a small nosegay arrangement to Angie. "Can't be having a wedding without flowers."

"You all are too wonderful. That does it, you have to come. I can't do this alone."

"To the wedding?" Libby asked.

Jenny nodded. "I need you all there."

"I'm not dressed for it," Max said.

"I think you are perfectly dressed just the way you are," Jenny said firmly.

Ten minutes later the entire staff of the Rocky Point Inn crowded into the judge's chambers. For the first time since the Inn had opened, it was locked up tight. Two of the guests had been given front door keys.

When they entered the chambers, Jenny's heart took wing when she saw Connor talking with the judge. He had shown up just as he'd said. Wearing a dark suit and snowy white shirt, he didn't resemble the man she'd known such a short time. If she'd thought about it, she would have expected the dark shirt and black leather jacket.

He looked startled at the small group that crowded in, then looked at Jenny. For a moment it was as if there were only the two of them in the room. He held her gaze as he crossed to her and reached out to take her hand. Raising it to his lips, he kissed her gently.

"Hi, Uncle Connor. Guess what, after

you marry Jenny, I can call her Auntie Jenny,'' Angie said in greeting.

''That you can,'' he concurred. ''Who decorated the cane so beautifully?''

''I did. Because today is special.'' Angie beamed up at them both.

''You did a terrific job. But Jenny won't need it for a few minutes. Want to hold it?'' He took it from Jenny and handed it to Angie. Then he wrapped her hand around his arm. ''Lean on me,'' he said softly as they walked slowly up to the judge.

Jenny almost cried. When had anyone told her to lean on him? If he never did another kind act, she would always remember his words. It was then Jenny knew she was falling in love with Connor Wolfe.

It was not the wedding she might have dreamed about as a teenager—had she given into such daydreams instead of practicing. It was more than what she'd expected over the last few years. The ceremony was solemn and hopeful. She was startled when Connor kissed her. The sensations roared through her like a tsunami. She wished she could have extended the kiss into the next millennium.

The cheers of her employees broke them

apart. The gleam in his eye promised more when they were alone.

"Auntie Jenny, Auntie Jenny, I get to hug you first," Angie said, tugging on Jenny's sleeve.

"Yes, you do," she said, turning to hug the little girl. Connor kept his hand firmly around her arm to steady her. For a moment she felt as if she could lean on him the rest of her life.

But it was only a temporary marriage—until Angie was grown. Enjoy it while she may, but never count on forever.

Despite Connor's misgivings, Brian had not shown. From what he'd said the last time Jenny had seen him, he had already headed back to San Diego.

Lunch was delicious. Sally had outdone herself with the tender roast beef and new potatoes. She'd even made a small wedding cake.

Jenny felt flushed with happiness throughout the meal. Her staff and friends had made the day special—on virtually no notice.

But the wedding night loomed. As the hours passed drawing closer and closer to the time she and Connor would enter her bedroom and shut the world away, she grew more and more apprehensive.

It was one thing for the worldly Connor—simply another woman to sleep with. But for Jenny it would be a first. She worried about the sight of the scars on her leg and hip. Would they repel him? What about her own lack of knowledge? Would that exasperate him? He was used to sophisticated women of the Pacific Rim. Instead he was getting a shy, damaged virgin from the backwaters of Maine.

Should she say something? Or just pretend?

The minutes ticked by and each one caused the butterflies in her stomach to flutter even more.

Upon learning about the wedding, Cilla's mother called and invited Angie to stay the weekend.

"You two aren't going away, I'm sure, with the February Festival starting. The least I can do is have her over here so you have some privacy," she'd said.

But when broached with the idea, Angie flatly refused.

"I thought Cilla was your friend," Connor said. Wasn't she the little girl that Angie played with every day after school?

"I don't want to go." Angie turned stubborn.

"It's all right. It was nice of Cilla's mom to invite you, but you don't have to go." Jenny gave her a hug and shook her head at Connor. "Do you want Cilla to come over here?"

Angie shook her head.

"Okay, then it's just you and me and Connor. We're a family now, so we'll start out that way. And tonight, before bed, we'll all have hot chocolate and tell each other the best part of our day."

"What was that about?" Connor asked a few minutes later when Angie went to get another helping of cake.

"She was spending the night at Cilla's when the fire broke out. I think she feels if she goes off again, this place will burn. I don't push her. Sooner or later she'll know that her leaving didn't cause the fire."

Connor looked at his niece, aware of the full undertaking he and Jenny were committing. Was he up to the task? He could do even more damage than losing her parents had already caused. Hell, he didn't know anything about raising a child.

But he did know what not to do. He'd learned that lesson well. He hadn't changed his mind about wanting to keep her away from his father. If nothing else, this new revelation convinced him they were doing the right thing. The last thing a child like Angie needed was a drunkard caring for her, leaving her alone for hours on end, expecting her to fend for herself. If she didn't want to visit at her friend's house, she never would have survived Brian's neglect.

Not that being married to Jenny would prove a hardship. Just looking at her had his anticipation cranking up a notch. He couldn't wait until it was the two of them alone in her room tonight. And all the nights that would follow.

Lunch had scarcely finished before Jenny had to deal with a problem with a new guest. Angie went to change and Connor went to get his things from the rental car. He hadn't brought much, just a few changes of clothes and his laptop. He'd started the procedure for relocating some of his senior staff, planning to leave several key people in Los Angeles to run things from that end.

He hesitated when he entered the private suite that belonged to Jenny. They were as legally married as any two people got, but he felt as if he were trespassing. Dumping his bag into her bedroom, he took the laptop and went back to the sitting area.

Looking around he took in the homey feel to the room—lacy curtains on the windows, colorful rugs scattered on the polished hardwood floor. The furnishings were comfortable. Quite a contrast to the super efficient, sterile lines in his condo.

''Hi, Uncle Connor. Want to come watch me skate?'' Angie asked, coming from her room. She had her skates over her shoulder, and was dressed warmly.

He glanced at his watch. Too late to take her to school, too early for her friends to be at the makeshift rink.

''I'll watch until your friends arrive.''

''I get to tell them all about the wedding. I wish my Mommy and Daddy could have come.''

''I'm sure they were watching from heaven,'' Connor said, hoping it was the right thing to say.

Angie's smile held sadness, but at least she was smiling.

When they reached the lobby, chaos prevailed. There were at least a half dozen couples milling around, suitcases and carry-on bags piled hither and yon. Libby,

Daniel and Jenny were behind the desk, helping new arrivals.

When she'd mentioned being fully booked up for the February Festival, she'd meant it. He was glad to be escaping to the relative quiet of the skating rink.

If anyone had ever asked how he'd spend his wedding day, if he'd ever thought to marry before learning about Angie, it wouldn't be watching an eight-year-old skate in the frozen north of Maine.

If things had been different, he would have swept his bride away to some warm locale—like the island in Tahiti from which he'd recently returned. They would have a quiet place all to themselves, not an Inn at the busiest time of year. He'd take her dining and dancing, slow songs that would let her snuggle up against him, so he could feel the soft curves, smell her fragrance.

Connor rubbed his hand across his face, trying to dispel the other images that came to mind for what he'd like to do with his new bride. He was sitting on a freezing bench, watching a child skate and he was getting as hot as sunshine thinking about Jenny, and their wedding night.

It might not be Tahiti, but they'd have privacy in her room. And a comfortable bed. And endless hours to forge bonds for this new relationship they'd both undertaken for Angie.

He checked his watch again, almost groaning when he calculated how many hours it would be until he and his wife could be alone. All the planning in the world hadn't prepared him for this waiting.

CHAPTER NINE

JENNY arranged for them to eat dinner in her suite that evening. With all the bustle with the guests, she knew they'd never have a quiet meal if she didn't distance herself. It might not be a bad idea to have a house away from the Inn. That way she could delegate to her staff and know they'd have to deal with things without coming to her for every little question.

Normally she loved being in the thick of things, but she knew it would be different with a family to consider.

For the first time in a decade, she had someone besides herself to take into account. And a house would offer more stability to Angie.

She had hired two temporary college workers to help with the overflow and one of them brought up the meals. Once they were eating, however, Jenny wondered if she should have stayed in the dining room.

Even with Angie, it seemed very intimate dining.

"I have something for you," Connor said when the plates had been cleared away.

"Oh, no. I didn't think about wedding gifts. I'm so sorry, Connor, I don't have anything for you." Jenny felt stricken. How could she have forgotten such a traditional token?

"It's not a wedding gift." He rose and crossed to the small desk and brought back a cell phone.

"You said you didn't know how to reach me. This is for you to carry around. I've programmed in my own cell number. All you need to do is press these two buttons and it'll find me."

"Can I try, Uncle Connor?" Angie asked, jumping up from her seat to see the phone.

"Sure." He caught himself. "If it's all right with Jenny, it's her phone."

"Let's see if you can work it," Jenny said. She felt a curious fluttering inside at Connor's thoughtfulness.

Angie pressed the buttons and a split second later, the phone in Connor's pocket trilled.

Angie grinned at her uncle. "Hello?"

He flipped it open and responded. She ran into the other room, talking constantly, obviously delighted with the new toy.

Jenny smiled. It was fun to watch them. To know they had already started building the bridge from past to future. If only it was as easy for her. She wished she could take Connor for what he was. He said he didn't mind her limp. That he did consider her responsible. She vowed never to let either down. Not like she had her father.

For a moment she remembered the happy days with her dad. They had been few and far between as she remembered.

"What's that frown for?" Connor asked, as he slipped the phone back into his pocket. "I thought it would be all right for her to call Cilla from the new phone."

"What? Oh, it is. I was just thinking."

"Regrets already?" he asked silkily.

"No. I was remembering my dad."

"I'm sorry he couldn't be here today to give you away."

"Odd isn't it? My dad's gone, but I wished so much he could have been here. You could have had yours and didn't want him. We didn't have a lot of fun times together, you know."

"You and your father?" Connor asked for clarification.

She nodded. "That was a nice thing to do with Angie. She's having a nice evening and is excited about our marriage and the new phone. I was trying to think about something similar in my life, but only practices and travel come to mind. It was hard training constantly. I don't feel I had that much fun."

"Why didn't you quit?"

She looked at him, horrified. "I couldn't have done that, it meant too much to my father."

"Children aren't here to live their parents' lives. You had a right to choose your own way."

"He sacrificed so much to enable me to compete, the least I could do was skate my best. Besides, look what happened the one time I tried something different."

"The accident was not your fault. It was merely a bad accident, lousy timing."

"Which wouldn't have happened if I'd followed orders and stayed in my room."

"Ground rules. Number one, don't dwell on the past. You can't change it, it's futile to think you could."

"What?"

"Number two, don't beat yourself up for mistakes. We all make them. Learn from them, don't repeat them, but don't relive them over and over until they become more important than they really are."

"Connor—"

"Rule number three—make plans, but don't cast them in concrete. Be flexible enough to revise if outside circumstances prevail. Rule four, live in today, but plan for the future."

She stared at him as he spoke. He meant every word he said. Was that how he had gotten beyond his own past? She grew fascinated. Who would have thought Connor Wolfe had *rules to live by?*

"How many rules do you have?" she asked.

"Enough to get to where I am today," he replied.

She rose and began to stack the dishes on the tray they'd come on. When the small table was cleared, she looked at it, then at Connor.

"Do you have a rule about helping your wife?"

He rose and took the tray. "Never needed one before, but I can make one."

He placed the tray on the hallway floor

near the wall, noticing another farther along.

Closing the door, he turned and looked at Jenny. Studying her for a moment, he smiled and said, "Another rule is exercise patience, things happen in their own time. But I'm having a hard time with that one right now."

Jenny felt the heat sweep through her. She felt as if she were on the edge of a precipice about to plunge over. There was a huge ticking clock, tolling the minutes until they went to bed. She was nervous as could be, but tried to hide it.

Should she ask him to wait, or bluff her way through? She couldn't hide behind Angie forever, but tonight she wanted her to stay up late.

Clearing her throat, she tried to smile. "Did you get your things unpacked?"

"I put my stuff in your room, but it's all still in the duffel."

"I cleared closet space and the top two drawers of the dresser. You might want to get another one entirely for your use."

"We can look at furniture when we find a house."

Angie came in and heard the last statement. "What house?" she asked warily.

"Your aunt Jenny and I will be looking for a nice big house for us to move to."

"No. I like it here." She looked at Jenny. "Can't we stay here?"

"It's a little small for three people," Jenny began.

"There's lots of rooms in the Inn. Connor can have one room and you and I can stay here."

Connor crossed to Angie and squatted down beside her. Their eyes met. "I'm not going to buy a house you don't like. And I'll make sure it's safe. It won't blow up, it won't burn and we'll be safe in that house. I promise you, Angie."

She studied him for a long moment, tears welling. "My house burned up with Mommy and Daddy. What if the new house burns up with you and Jenny?"

"It won't, I promise you. We'll make sure we don't have a propane tank for starters. And we'll have smoke alarms in every room. We'll buy brick, it won't burn. I won't let anything happen to you, I promise."

"You are going to be a terrific father," Jenny said sometime later when Angie was asleep.

Connor looked at her in surprise. They were in her room, putting away the few items of clothing he'd brought. He had the definite feeling Jenny was stalling, but he wasn't going to wait much longer.

"Why would you say that."

"You knew instinctively what her fear was. I didn't. And you allayed them. You cared how she was feeling and did what you could to make her feel safe and loved."

"Anyone would do the same."

"Did your father for you?"

He paused. "No."

"See, you have already passed him by a mile."

"So I might make a good father, what about husband?"

"Do you want to be a good husband?" she whispered. Hope fluttered. Maybe he was beginning to have warm feelings for her. If he wanted to expand the terms of their agreement, she was all for it.

"We're getting hitched for a long time. Don't you think it would be better to get along than not?" he asked.

Turning away to hide the shaft of disappointment, she nodded. How foolish to think he cared anything for her beyond a casual friendship. Their marriage was for Angie.

"Which side of the bed do you want me to take?" he asked.

She turned around. Connor was leaning against the wall, his arms crossed over his chest. He looked completely at ease, as if they were discussing the February Festival. Heat licked through her veins. She glanced at the bed.

"I never thought about it," she said. "Whichever side you want, I guess."

"Don't you have a favorite?"

"I usually pretty much sleep in the middle."

"How about when you, ah, have friends over."

She looked at him. Oh, God, she couldn't do this. Swallowing hard, she took a breath.

"I don't have friends over," she said.

"Since you have had Angie here, you mean?"

She shook her head.

He pushed off from the wall and crossed the room. Jenny watched every step. When he was close enough to touch, he reached out and placed his warm hands on her shoulders, tugging her a bit closer.

"You go to their places?"

She shook her head, her gaze never leaving his.

He studied her for a long moment.

"So how often exactly do you make love with a man?"

"Counting tonight? It'll be one."

He leaned his forehead against hers and closed his eyes with a groan. "You're a virgin," he said so softly she wasn't sure she was meant to hear.

"If that's a problem we can hold off," she said quickly.

"Oh, no, honey, that's no problem." Connor tilted her head back and kissed her.

Jenny felt her knees give way and would have collapsed in a puddle of molten sensations if Connor hadn't wrapped his arms around her and held her close.

His mouth explored hers, his tongue moving against hers in an age-old dance of seduction.

She reveled in the elementary awareness of each touch, each brush of fingertips against her back, of lips moving against hers, of the feeling of spinning away from gravity and moving into the realm of rainbows.

He trailed kisses along her cheek, down

to her jaw. Jenny knew she'd been kissed before, but memory was fleeting, she could only feel Connor, taste him. No other kiss had ever come close.

"Maybe we should turn off the lights," she said, trying to fight the wave of panic that threatened as her emotions grew.

He lifted his head and gazed down into her eyes. "I'm not going to do a thing you don't want."

"Maybe. But I think I'd like the lights off."

He took two steps, swept his hand down against the switch plunging them into darkness. Before she could draw breath, he was back.

"Better?"

"Thank you." She felt foolish, scared, thrilled.

When his fingers began to tug her sweater over her head, she assisted. Then let her own hands brush down his chest to the bottom of his shirt. Pulling it up, she couldn't take it off. Frustration rose.

"I'm not as experienced at this as you," she said.

She heard a chuckle and the shirt was gone. Her hands pressed against his hot skin, feeling the taut muscles, the brush of chest hair. Fascinated, she explored.

They were scarcely more than strangers, but she was drawn to him as never to anyone before. When he touched her she felt beautiful. When he kissed her she forgot her own name. And when he finally made her his, she wanted the moment to last through eternity.

No wonder people love to make love, Jenny thought drowsily a little later. She had never felt so close to another individual before. She loved Connor. Should she tell him? Or would he only scoff? She felt as if her heart would burst with emotions, but knew he viewed their liaison as only a way to provide a home for Angie and to keep her from his father.

Could she make him fall in love with her over the years? Or would he be content to go his own way once Angie was grown?

She could scarcely hold that thought. Look to the future, he'd said. To her it looked like heartbreak on the horizon.

"You okay?" he asked, shifting, pulling her closer, covering them with the duvet.

"Never better." It was true. Purposely she relinquished the fear for the future.

Right now, this moment, she felt cherished. Had she ever felt that way before? Thinking about it, she knew she had not. Could the night last forever?

Connor awoke first the next morning. It was still early, dark outside. But he was wide-awake and knew he wouldn't be going back to sleep. Easing himself out of the bed, he tried not to wake Jenny. He tucked the covers around her and headed for the bathroom.

He tried not to think about the gift she'd given him, but couldn't get over discovering she'd never slept with a man before. It made him take extra care, make sure everything had been perfect for her first time. Who would have thought one day he'd be married and probably to the last virgin in Maine?

How could she have gone so long without some man persuading her? But as he considered it, he knew. Her father had kept her on a tight schedule. She probably hadn't dated much as a teenager. Then the years of rehab after the accident would have made relationships the last thing she wanted. Especially with her view of herself courtesy of her father and ex-partner.

Last night had proved her to be a passionate woman, not afraid to try new things, or to give her all. If it hadn't been her first time, he would have wakened her in the night when he awoke, and made love all over again.

Dressing, he slipped out of the suite and headed for the kitchen. It was too early to expect breakfast, but he'd bet Sally Thompson was already at work. He had work himself to do. Later today he wanted to start house hunting. And keep some distance from Jenny. This wasn't some happy-ever-after soppy story. It was a business deal to provide for Angie. He couldn't get too comfortable or too complaisant. He wasn't cut out to be family material, he knew that and he had better keep it in the forefront of his mind.

The afterglow of her wedding night soon faded as the responsibilities and minor problems with running an Inn came full spate on Saturday. The February Festival had started, her rooms were full with a waiting list to boot. And people kept calling at the last moment hoping for cancellations.

The weather was perfect, in the low twenties, so the ice sculptures would hold.

Yet the sun shone, casting a million sparkles on the snow and giving the appearance of warmth despite the low temperatures.

She loved the excitement surrounding the festival. The college kids had the week excused from classes to more fully participate. People from all over the Northeast came to participate in the sculpturing contests. And the big ball at the end had been planned since last year's event.

Jenny had never gone to the ball, but she wondered if Connor would want to go this year.

When she had a break, she ran up to the suite, hoping to find him. She hadn't seen him since she awoke this morning. He wasn't there. Neither was Angie, but she knew she'd gone with Andrew and his family for the fun in the park. Had Connor gone with them? For a moment she felt a pang. She had to work. Normally she enjoyed the hectic pace of February. But today she felt rebellious. She wanted to be with Connor and Angie enjoying the festival. For once she'd like to have no responsibilities—to be able to wander about like any other tourist, having fun, spending time with her new family. Making happy memories.

As she slowly made her way back down the stairs she knew nothing had changed by getting married. At least not yet.

Connor watched her come down the stairs. She looked tired. A glance around the empty lobby had him wondering what had happened to last night's crowd. Or the one he'd seen before he left this morning. Out around town, he suspected. Traffic had approached that of L.A. when he'd tried to drive through the center of Rocky Point. Everyone he'd seen had been gawking at the various ice sculptures growing in almost every flat spot.

He crossed to the bottom step before she reached it. When she did, she paused, her eyes level with his. Did he imagine the spark of delight that flared?

"Want to go see them carving ice sculptures?" he asked.

"Oh, I wish I could. But I can't just leave the Inn," she said, genuine regret showing.

He glanced at the front desk. That young man who worked afternoons was already there, leafing through a magazine. There was no one else in the vicinity.

"Got your cell phone?" he asked, turning back to Jenny.

"Yes."

Nodding his head toward the desk, he said, "Give him the number. He can call you in an emergency. This isn't L.A. We can be back here from anywhere in Rocky Point in a matter of minutes. Where's Angie?"

"She went with Andrew and his parents. She won't be back until after dinner."

"Then it's just you and me, babe," he said. "Come and show me what your town's got."

"I'll need a jacket."

He eyed her wool slacks, the sturdy, warm boots she already wore. Her sweater was pale pink, making her look pretty as a picture. He scowled. He was here for a tour of the town, not to think how Jenny looked. Getting sloppily sentimental about things never got him anywhere.

"Where is it?" he asked, hoping she didn't have to climb the stairs. He couldn't help worrying about the difficulty she had walking, though he'd never say anything to her. But in this day and age, shouldn't something be done about the discomfort?

"In my office."

In only moments they were on their way. The big, black sports utility vehicle was only one of two cars in the parking lot. He helped Jenny in and they took off.

Just like a couple who had been together for years, instead of only one night, he thought as he turned toward town. He didn't like the trend of his thoughts. He was too old to fall for fairy tale endings. They had married for Angie, nothing more.

His cell phone rang. Flipping it open, he heard Stephanie at the other end.

"Things are better, boss, but when are you coming back?" she asked.

Connor glanced at the people walking along the sidewalks, bundled up to their noses against the cold. He took in the industrious work of those carving ice designs, of the laughing children running around, pelting each other with snowballs. The scene was as alien to him as landing on the moon would have been. But something tugged at his heart. He wanted to stay.

"Not for a while. Did Harry get all those documents for me?" For several moments they discussed the crises he'd averted on his brief trip there. When they wound down, Stephanie said, "I'm going home and enjoying the rest of the weekend. When you get in on Monday, you and I need to talk.''

''Sounds ominous.''

''Don't freeze before you get back here,'' she said with a laugh.

He shut off the phone and put it back in his pocket.

''Problems?''

''Ongoing ones. Nothing I can't handle.''

''But you'll be heading for L.A. again soon.''

''When I have to for business.''

He found a parking place. Shutting off the engine he looked at Jenny. ''Do you have a problem with that?''

''It depends. Is this how this marriage works? You spend weekends here and the week on the West Coast?''

''I'm planning to move my base of operations here. Once that's accomplished my trips to the West Coast should be few and far between.'' Connor didn't like explaining himself to anyone. He hadn't had to do it much in his life. Was this another change because of marriage?

''Do you want to go with me when I go?'' he asked.

"No. I'm thinking of Angie. I thought we wanted to give her stability. Your being gone isn't going to do much toward that end."

"I won't be gone much. You'll probably be sick to death of me before long."

"I doubt that," she said, smiling at him.

Connor felt as if a weight had lifted. Her smile was dangerous to a man who had been alone all his life.

"Come on, you can tell me all about ice sculptures," he said. In only a moment they joined the people on the sidewalk wandering along, watching as the ice formations took shape, commenting, critiquing.

"Ever want to do one on the Inn's yard?" he asked at one point.

"We did for a couple of years running. But it's harder than it looks, requires more skill than any of my staff possesses. And we are on the edge of town, so off the beaten track. These homes are perfectly situated."

"Did Cathy ever do one?"

"She helped when we did the ones at the Inn. Gosh, Angie was just a toddler then, I wonder if she even remembers. It would be something to tell her about her mother. We need to make sure we talk about her folks, so she won't forget them. I don't have many memories of my mother, you know. Dad rarely spoke about her after she died. Do you remember your mother?''

''Nothing good.''

''That's so sad. Cathy didn't have happy memories either. We need to make sure Angie does.''

''It doesn't sound as if yours are all that great,'' Connor said. They had stopped near a used bookstore. Inside patrons were wandering around. To one side there was a coffee bar.

''Want something hot to drink?''

She nodded. Slowly they made their way inside. ''You need a warmer jacket, Connor,'' she said as they waited for their beverages. ''There's a nice store down the block. Let's see if we can find something in black for you.''

He raised an eyebrow. ''Something in black?''

''You seem to wear it all the time. I think of it as your signature color.''

''My what?''

She smiled, her eyes dancing in amusement. She was teasing him, he realized with a start. Had anyone teased him since he was a kid and Lefty Monohan had teased him in school? Somehow this felt vastly different from Lefty's brand.

"Would you like bright blue? Or how about orange?"

"Orange would make me look like a highway worker. I'll stick with black."

"Told you," she said.

Connor found himself wanting to see her smile again, to hear her laugh. He wasn't one for attachments or drawing close to another person. He had casual friends, and had had several relationships over the years, but never close ones. And no one teased him.

They found a jacket—black as Jenny predicted—and headed back for the Inn to be there when Angie returned. Connor went to the suite to check his email and work while Jenny stayed downstairs to assist the front desk crew as people returned for the various events of the Festival, or prepared to depart for evening activities.

When Jenny went upstairs to tuck Angie in bed sometime later, she was feeling the strain of a full Inn and being married to a man she hardly knew. Things were not going exactly as she'd thought they would, not that she had had long to ponder the situation. It was early days. It would take time to feel like a couple, to do things as a family.

Tomorrow, Connor had suggested they take Angie around with them. Jenny wasn't sure if it was to appeal to Angie or to keep a buffer between them. Ever since they'd bought that jacket, he seemed to be drawing away. Had she said something to offend him? She couldn't think of anything.

Now it was almost time to go to bed. Jenny felt even more keyed up than she had last night. Tonight she knew what to expect. Would Connor want to make love again?

She was disappointed to find the sitting room empty when she entered. Checking on Angie, she tucked the covers in snugly and kissed her forehead. Once again she vowed to her friend Cathy that she would cherish her child.

''We're doing what we can for your little girl,'' she whispered, her heart aching for the loss of her friend, and all she'd miss of Angie's growing up.

When Jenny entered her own room, it, too, was empty. Where was Connor?

She hadn't seen him downstairs, but

there were some people still in the dining room, just talking and drinking coffee. Maybe he'd joined them.

She prepared for bed and slid beneath the cool sheets, waiting for them to warm up. Had she done something wrong last night that Connor didn't want to sleep with her again? Rolling to her side, she drifted off to sleep, wondering if she'd ever make love with her husband again.

Some time later she was awakened by a warm body behind hers, lips brushing across her cheek.

"Connor?" she asked sleepily.

"Who else would you expect in your bed?" he asked in a mock growl.

Jenny smiled and turned on her back, wishing she could see him, but the room was dark.

"Where were you?"

"I got to talking with some people in the dining room. I didn't realize how late it was." His hands began to caress. His mouth found hers in the darkness. Once again Jenny was caught up in the flare of passion Connor had taught her.

CHAPTER TEN

THE next week proved to be one of the happiest Jenny remembered. She was busy at the Inn with a full complement of guests. But there was time to steal away and participate in some of the activities of the Festival once Angie was home from school.

Connor spent each morning working with his West Coast office, then would take off to search for office space, and a home.

By the time Angie returned from school each day, Connor and Jenny were ready to take a break and focus on the little girl.

Angie blossomed under the adult attention. She seemed less sad and unhappy. Jenny knew it would be years before the child got over her parents' death, if ever, but at least she felt they were making strides to show Angie she would be safe with them.

They watched as people made the most amazing ice sculptures. Bought snow cones. Critiqued Angie when she made snow angels and cheered her on when she won a prize for her age group.

Trying to maintain a sense of normalcy, Jenny insisted they eat dinner alone in the suite, rather than in the crowded, hectic dining room. This gave them time to share as a family.

The first night, Angie chattered freely, telling Jenny and Connor about her day in school, the fun she'd had walking along to see the festivities. Jenny commented from time to time, but she was more aware of Connor sitting opposite her, watching them both with an intensity that surprised her. When she tried to get him to contribute, his comments were short and to the point.

By the third evening, however, he joined in with Angie, teasing her gently. Jenny wondered briefly if his reticence during the earlier meals came from not sharing in family life before. The picture he painted of his father was certainly bleak.

"So tell us about your office search," Jenny said on Thursday evening.

"Not much to tell. I haven't found anything in Rocky Point that I want. I may have to look further afield."

''Like where, Stanburg? It's the next town, but not as large as Rocky Point.''

''If needs be. Tomorrow Darryl is showing me some houses that might be suitable to renovate into office space. If I don't see anything tomorrow, then I'll widen the search. I haven't found anything I want to buy for a home for us, either.''

''You're looking, without me?'' Jenny asked, taken aback. She thought they'd search for their new home together.

''I'm only eliminating totally unsuitable houses. If I find one that meets our criteria, then of course I'd make sure you saw it before making a decision.''

''What are criteria?'' Angie asked.

''Things we want in a house,'' Jenny explained. ''Remember, Uncle Connor said we'd look for a brick house.''

''So no matter who huffs and puffs, it won't fall down,'' Angie said.

''Exactly,'' Jenny said with a smile.

''If my daddy's house had been brick, it wouldn't have burned down, would it?'' Angie asked in a small voice. ''But sticks and straw don't make good houses.''

''Oh, honey, don't think like that. The fire was a terrible accident, it didn't happen just because you had a frame house.''

"What are you talking about?" Connor asked.

"The three pigs," Jenny said, reaching out to brush the hair back from Angie's face. "Your Uncle Connor will get us a terrific house. And it won't burn down."

She glanced at Connor. He looked puzzled.

"What three pigs?"

"The nursery story, The Three Little Pigs."

He resumed eating. "I never had fairy tales."

"As a child?"

He looked at her. "Do you really picture my father reading nursery rhymes?"

Jenny's heart constricted. He'd never even had a childhood. He'd been foraging around on his own all his life. Her anger toward Brian rose. How dare the man treat his own child the way he had. And how dare he propose to take his granddaughter and expose her to the same kind of home life.

Jenny began to understand the magnitude of Connor's plan. He didn't know how to be a father, to be part of a family, yet he'd risked it all to provide for a niece he'd never met before this month.

And took on a woman he'd never met into the bargain.

"Tell you what," Jenny said when dinner was finished. "After your bath, Angie, we can have you tell Uncle Connor all about the three little pigs. They don't tell these stories in California, so it'll be the first time he's heard it."

"A gap in my education?" Connor asked smoothly.

"Absolutely. And maybe we'll find some others we can remedy."

She wanted to get away before she grew sloppily nostalgic. No matter how driven her dad had been as she got older, she had happy memories of her younger years. And the driving need to achieve hadn't all been one-sided. She'd strived for years to succeed. It hadn't been her father's fault that just when the gold was in reach she'd been in the accident.

No more than it was her fault. She had to remember that. But the old guilt was hard to expunge.

Jenny let Connor put Angie to bed. She wanted to give them as much time together as possible to build a bond that would last forever. Beside, with all the afternoons she'd been taking off, the paperwork was piling up.

It was after eleven when she finished and left the office. The lobby was deserted. Ben Harrington was behind the desk, working on a college assignment. When there was nothing needed for the desk clerk job, Jenny didn't mind the students working on other tasks.

She was about to head upstairs when she noticed Connor standing on the porch, under the glare of the outside light.

It was freezing out and he was there in his shirt sleeves. Didn't he feel the cold?

She grabbed her jacket and headed outside.

"Connor, what are you doing out here without a jacket?"

He turned, amusement in his gaze. "Checking up on me?"

"Well, if you act like you don't have the sense God gave a mongoose, then yes, I guess I am. Aren't you freezing?"

"I just stepped out a minute ago. I've been having a discussion with some of your guests. Thought I'd get a bit of air before going to bed."

Casually, he reached out and drew her closer, resting his arm across her shoulders.

He turned to look back toward the darkness beyond the porch light.

"Is everything all right?" she asked softly. For the first time, she felt married. This is what husbands and wives did, discussed things, shared problems, spent quiet moments together at the end of a day.

"Sure."

They stood in silence for a moment.

"Maybe not," he said.

"What?"

"I thought I had it all figured. Get married, keep Angie from my father. But the truth is, Jenny, I think I stepped in where I don't belong. I don't know anything about being a father. Hell, I don't even know stories an eight-year-old knows."

"Connor, your ability as a father doesn't rest on storytelling."

"Of course not, but it's representative. I didn't have a normal upbringing. I don't know how to raise a child."

"Neither do most parents. Kids don't come with instruction booklets. We'll just do the best we can."

"You think my father did his best?"

She shook her head. "No. But you are not like him."

"I've got his blood in my veins."

"And your mother's and all the other ancestors before you. Plus you have your own unique experiences and values. I think you're going to make a great father."

There was a pause.

"How about a husband?" he asked softly.

"There you have an advantage. No booklet, but I can tell you what to do."

He tightened his grip slightly. "Only if you stop acting afraid around me."

Jenny looked up at him. "I'm not afraid of you, Connor."

"You act skittish anytime I get near you."

She swallowed. "That's not fear. It's…awareness," she finished in a whisper.

He looked into her eyes, slowly turning until he faced her. "So you have to pull back?"

"That or jump your bones," she said, desperately hoping he wouldn't laugh at her.

He groaned softly and pulled her into his arms. His kiss was fierce and short.

"I've been waiting for the night you tell me you have a headache, or something," he said.

"That'll probably never come," she said. Was it true? Had he thought her *afraid* of him? She'd tried so hard not to show her feelings, to keep something to herself for fear of his turning away. If she was afraid of anything, it was of wanting him too much.

"Then let's go upstairs and I'll do my best to be a good husband."

If Jenny thought her revelation would make things easier between them, she was doomed to disappointment. Friday morning Connor was as distant and withdrawn as the other mornings. Was that his normal personality, or was he still keeping a lock on his own emotions?

He found her mid morning in the dining room just finishing a discussion of the dinner menu with Sally Thompson.

"Did you need something?" she asked as Sally headed back to the kitchen. The last of the breakfast dishes had been cleared, and several of the tables already set for dinner.

"I just heard there's a dance at the college tomorrow night. The grand finale of the festival. The awards for the sculptures will be given. I take it we can see them posted by the ice sculptures on Sunday.''

''Yes. And by Monday, the town pretty much gets back to normal for another year. Only the melting designs remind us for a few days of the festival.''

''Shall we take in the dance?''

''Connor, I don't dance.''

''Why not? You can walk fine.''

''I do not. I limp, need a cane.''

''You won't need a cane, I'll hold you. Spread your wings and come with me, Jenny,'' he said.

She was tempted. She couldn't remember the last time she'd gone to a dance. It had been on one of the World Tours, she thought. Dare she attend this one?

She looked at Connor. He knew how she walked. He knew her limitations. If he wanted to go, wanted to take her, why not?

''Okay. I'd like that,'' she said, already wondering what in the world she'd wear.

''Angie can stay the night at Cilla's. It's all arranged.''

''What? Connor, she hadn't slept over at Cilla's since her parents died. She won't do it.''

''She's already agreed.''

''How did you manage that miracle?''

''Logically.''

''Oh right, like an eight-year-old is big on logic.''

He shrugged. ''That and bribery.''

''What did you promise her?''

''That she could call us right before she went to bed. That Cilla's mother would get her up early and bring her right back here so we could all have breakfast together. And I promised the Inn wouldn't burn down.''

''And she believed you, just like that? I've told her that over and over.''

''Ah, but you didn't point out the propane tank her folks had caused the accident. The Inn is on the city's gas main. Big difference.''

Jenny couldn't believe it was that simple.

''I also told her at any time during the night, I'd come get her if she wanted to come home.''

Jenny loved attending the February Festival Finale. She had yearned for years to see what it was like, hearing wonderful things from her guests who attended. And it upheld all the promise. The ballroom at the college had been decorated in silver and white, continuing a snowy theme. The dresses worn were lovely, and Jenny felt young again wearing the new dress she and Libby had found that morning. A deep cranberry color, it fit like a dream. She loved the feeling of femininity it gave. The appreciative glances from Connor went a long way to making the evening one she would not soon forget.

And best of all, when they returned home, it was to a message from Cilla's mother that Angie and Cilla had gone to sleep with no trouble and she expected them to sleep through the night.

When Jenny came from the bathroom sometime later, ready for bed, Connor watched her. He was leaning against the headboard, the sheet and duvet covering him from the waist down. She knew he wore nothing to bed, and couldn't help the excitement that washed through her.

"You're limping more than usual. Does your leg hurt?" he asked.

"A bit. But it's worth it. I had such a great time tonight. Thank you for taking me."

"A small enough thing. Climb into bed and I'll rub your leg for you."

"I'll be fine."

"Sore muscles make it harder to sleep. Come on, climb in."

She complied and lay back. He moved to gently rub her thigh and hip, easing the tight muscles, soothing.

"Where did you learn this technique?" she asked, feeling the pain ease away.

"Picked up here and there. Guys play sports, get hurt. Can't always afford a doctor." His hands were warm, firm, soothing, caressing.

"Did you find the place you wanted for your office," she asked. He hadn't said. Slowly Jenny closed her eyes. With the pain in her leg easing, she was getting very tired. It was later than her normal bedtime and she'd been on the go since before six.

"There is one possible. Want to ride out to see it tomorrow?"

"Ummm." She felt as if she were floating on air. Slowly Jenny drifted to sleep.

She awoke the next morning to Angie plunging into the room.

"I stayed all night at Cilla's!" she said excitedly. Jenny sat up sleepily. Connor's spot on the bed was empty. How late was it?

"I see you did. Did you have fun?"

"Yes. And maybe Cilla can come here to spend the night next weekend."

"I don't see why not." Jenny gave her a hug. "I want to hear all about your sleepover. Connor will want to hear it too, so you can tell us at breakfast. Where is Connor?"

"He came to get me. He's downstairs drinking coffee. He told me to come get you so we can eat and then go see where he might have an office. He got the key for today. Hurry up, Auntie Jenny. I'm hungry!"

Jenny hurried.

After breakfast, Connor took them on a drive through the town, stopping at each award winner of the ice-sculpting contest. The town was still full of visitors, but already almost half had checked out of the Inn. By Monday afternoon, the visitors would have left and Rocky Point would be back to normal.

After the last statue had been viewed, he headed to a side street and stopped in front of a huge old house. Nondescript, needing paint and yard work, it stood apart from its neighbors. It was two stories tall, with large windows and a wide front porch.

"This is the best Darryl had to offer," he said, studying the place.

"Probably not what you're used to," Jenny said. To her it looked like it would take a lot of work to make it viable. How much time and money did he want to put into something like this? Would he reconsider moving part of his operations here? What if he insisted they move to California?

He shrugged. "Our administrative offices are in a high rise building on Wilshire Boulevard. Glass and concrete. Nothing like this."

"What's the inside like?" Jenny asked brightly. She didn't want him to change his mind. Could she do anything to influence his decision? Maybe the inside was in better shape.

It wasn't.

"What's that smell?" Angie asked, exploring the large room they first entered.

"When a house has been closed up for a long time, it gets a musty smell," Jenny explained. "It needs to be aired out."

"And probably gutted." Connor looked around at the water stain on the ceiling, the peeling wallpaper on one corner.

"If it leaked to this ceiling, what does the upstairs room look like?" she asked.

"This was from a bath overflow, the roof is sound. About the only thing that is, I think." He wandered through the rooms, studying them with a critical eye. Jenny's hopes dropped. If this was the best Rocky Point had to offer new businesses, no wonder it wasn't exactly expanding by leaps and bounds.

"I've seen enough," he said a few moments later.

Jenny was silent on the ride back to the real estate office where Connor dropped off the key. She was certain it didn't meet the image he had for his company.

When they returned to the Inn, Angie headed out to go ice skating with her friends. Jenny went to check on things in the kitchen. When she returned a few moments later, she saw Connor engaged with two of her guests. The three men seemed to be having a serious discussion.

She veered to the front desk where Libby was working.

"How are things going?"

"Good. We've had most of the guests check out with no fuss. Five couples are scheduled to check out in the morning.

Leaving only Mrs. Abercrombie in room sixteen. It'll seem dead here next week in comparison,'' Libby said.

''I know, but I can use the breather. We have a lot of rooms booked for spring break.''

Libby nodded toward Connor and the other men. ''I have to say that surprised me.''

''What?''

''His talking with some of the guests. He always seems too intense to me to casually start up a conversation.''

Jenny watched them all for a moment. ''I think all three of them are that way. Maybe like draws to like. These men aren't like most of the guests who are content to enjoy the quieter pace of Rocky Point.''

''You're right—they all have that cut-throat approach to life.''

Jenny grinned at her friend. ''Hardly cut-throat. Just driven, I think. Maybe we can play that up. Even if you are a Type-A personality, we have something for you at The Rocky Point Inn.''

''I don't, somehow, see Connor letting himself be advertised as an attraction of the Inn,'' Libby said dryly.

Jenny shook her head smiling at the picture in her mind. "Definitely not. I could never let him know!"

After Angie had gone to bed, Jenny and Connor sat in the sitting room. It had been a lovely day. She wished it could continue, but it was getting late.

"Your leg bothering you?" Connor asked as he sprawled back in the chair, his legs stretched out in front of him.

"No. Maybe I've missed the boat not going for massage somewhere. There's not a sports clinic here, but I've heard of them. I thought they were just trendy. But if they can do what you did last night, they're well worth it."

"I still think you should check with your doctor about the problem."

"Next time I see him, I will." Jenny leaned back on the cushions. "I'm sorry there's no suitable office space for you to relocate. I never thought much about availability before."

"No reason for you to do so. Where did you live when you were a kid?"

"Over the garage my dad owned. It was a small apartment, but the only home I knew until I got this place."

He looked at her for a long moment.

"Amazing, you've lived in the same town all your life, and only two different homes. I've lived in so many apartments, they all blur together. Before I went out on my own, the longest stretch in one place was two years."

"What about school?"

"I changed a lot."

Jenny considered how different their childhoods had been, yet neither had been average.

"I hope we can provide better for Angie," she said.

"If she stays here, she'll have grown up in one town like you."

"But not with the endless practice, or the traveling to meets and all. I don't feel I have a lot of friends my age since I missed a lot of school while competing."

"It's a tough life, but you must have been quite good to be on the Olympic team," he said.

"Sometimes I wonder what things would be like if I hadn't been so good. If my dad hadn't pushed so much," she said pensively.

"What would you change?"

"I'd have more friends. Feel more a part of the community. I would have partied

more, dated, explored being a kid.'' She
took a breath. The past was gone. Nothing
would change it. But she would never push
her children to a goal for her sake like her
father had done. Her children?

She looked at Connor as if afraid he
could read minds. Nothing had been said
about children in this marriage.

''Enough talk of the past. It's the present, I'm interested in. Time for bed,''
Connor said, rising and holding out his
hand.

She put hers into it and rose. He was
right—the present was much more fun than
thinking about the past

When they were in their bedroom, the
door firmly shutting out the world, Connor
placed his palms against her cheeks,
threading his fingers through the softness
of her hair.

''I want you, Jenny.''

She gazed into his dark eyes, seeing the
desire reflected. ''I want you, too,'' she
said softly, wishing with an ache that he
could offer words she wanted to hear.

She felt the control he exerted on his
emotions as he slowly kissed her. He was
such an intense individual. Yet had remark-
able self control.

When he drew her sweater over her head, the air chilled. But she knew now that in only moments he would warm her like no one else ever had.

Their lovemaking was explosive. Sometimes it was slow and languid, others fast and furious. Tonight it seemed all the more special after a perfect day. Jenny thought her heart would burst with happy delight. She loved this man and would all her days.

He kissed her and gathered her close to him. Covering them both, he seemed to settle in for the night.

"I love you," she said softly.

He stiffened. She knew he'd heard her. Sighing softly, Jenny turned slightly, trying to see him in the darkness.

"Don't worry, it doesn't come with strings attached." She hadn't really thought he'd reciprocate, despite a faint hope that had been there.

"You're just caught up in passion. People think they need to say something like that," he growled.

"No, I'm not caught up in the moment. I've felt this way for days. I wanted to tell you. So I did. It's no big deal, Connor. I certainly didn't mean to get you wrought up over it. I was hoping you'd like to know how I felt. Go to sleep.''

When Jenny awoke in the morning, Connor had gone.

CHAPTER ELEVEN

CONNOR lay on his back staring at the ceiling, seeing nothing in the predawn darkness. He'd been awake for at least an hour. Since leaving Maine three weeks ago, he'd not slept through the night once.

First of all he was a damned coward. Jenny had spoken of love and he'd bolted like a scared rabbit. He closed his eyes, but the words echoed. He wished she'd told him in the light of day so he could have seen her eyes. But it had been dark, like now.

He'd never had anyone tell him they loved him before.

Did she mean it? Or had it been passion talking?

What was he going to do about it? What was there to do about it. If she imagined herself in love, so be it. It meant nothing to him.

But he missed her. Missed her and Angie. They'd spoken on the phone almost daily, but it wasn't the same. A few moments hearing her voice only made him yearn that much more to be with her. Watch her as she walked. See her hair brush her shoulders. Say something to cause her to smile and watch her eyes light up.

He could go back. He'd planned to relocate his headquarters there. Nothing had changed. Once he found a place, he'd start the move. But in three weeks, he had not made much progress.

Connor frowned. It wasn't like him. He normally focused on a problem, found a solution and implemented it.

Lately he'd spent too much time remembering Jenny. And hearing her words echo over and over.

He needed to do something—only he didn't know what exactly. After years of being on his own, of being focused on his goals, he was stymied. What did he say to someone who loved him?

And for how long would that love last? Until he did something to screw it up, probably.

His phone rang. He glanced at the clock, it wasn't even five yet. Normally he wouldn't be awake for another hour.

"Wolfe," he said, answering it before it rang again.

"Uncle Connor, can you come?" Angie's frantic voice sounded across the miles. "We need you. Someone smashed our car and Auntie Jenny isn't moving. There's blood and broken glass and everything. Can you come help us?"

He sat up, fear shafting through him.

"Angie, where are you? What happened?"

"I think I got hurted too. My arm hurts and there's blood on my jacket. When Auntie Jenny didn't answer, I got that phone you gave her, and I called you just like you showed me. Oh, here comes the sheriff, can you hear the siren?"

"Angie, listen to me. Tell me what happened." He rose, flicked on the light and began to get dressed.

"Auntie Jenny was taking me to school and some old car smashed into us. She hit her head, I think. Anyway she's not awake."

"Oh God," he said softly. "Is the sheriff there?"

"It's Sheriff Tucker. He doesn't look glad to see us. Can you come, Uncle

Connor? We miss you. I'm scared.'' She started to cry.

"Okay, honey, calm down. I'm on my way. But Angie, it'll take a while. You do what Sheriff Tucker tells you to."

"'Kay." The connection was cut off.

"Damn." He punched in the number and heard it ring. But no one answered.

Connor was airborne within the next two hours. He tried the cell phone again, and when it hadn't worked, he'd called the Inn. They hadn't heard of the accident, knew nothing, and wanted to ring off so they could call the sheriff's department and find out what happened.

Connor got the sheriff department's number and called there himself. The first time, before he boarded the jet headed for Boston, he'd been given to dispatch, which knew only that the sheriff had been called to an accident.

An interminable hour later, he reached one of the deputies.

"Bunch of kids driving the other car. Going too fast and hit a patch of ice. Slammed right into Jenny's car," the deputy said once Connor identified himself.

"How is my wife?"

"Took her to hospital. I haven't heard

any updates. They are still working to get the cars cleared off the road.''

Connor obtained the hospital's number, disconnected and dialed immediately. He couldn't imagine what Jenny was feeling. It was close to a repeat of what happened so many years ago—the accident that changed her life. What must be going through her mind right now?

He hoped this one didn't prove as serious. What would he do if she was severely injured? After only a few short days with her, he couldn't imagine his life without her in it. Don't let any harm come to her, he prayed.

Connor felt he'd lived in total frustration forever. The person he spoke with in Admitting at the hospital didn't have any information, Jenny was in the emergency room. He tried to be patient, but it was his wife injured, and he wanted some answers. He was transferred, but there was no report. Try back in a few minutes, they suggested.

He called Stephanie and instructed her to rent a plane for him from Boston to Portland. He wasn't waiting for some commuter plane and then driving a couple of hours. He needed to get to Rocky Point as fast as possible.

The hours seemed endless. The reports too sketchy to be of help.

Finally he reached Libby.

"How is she?" If he could get out and push the plane, he would have done so.

"Jenny is being held overnight as a precaution. She has a slight concussion and they want to monitor it. Angie needed four stitches in her arm. But she's here with us now. In the kitchen with Sally actually. Do you want to talk to her?"

"Yes." Thank God. They were both going to be all right. It seemed as if the weight of the world lifted. Connor felt an emotion he'd never experienced before. He gazed out the plane window, hoping he didn't do something stupid like cry!

"Hi, Uncle Connor."

"Angie, how are you, sweetheart?"

"I got stitches in my arm. And I had glass in my hair! And in my clothes. I had to change. And I didn't even go to school today. But I can't go skating this afternoon neither. Libby said I have to rest. So Mrs. Thompson is making brownies. I really, really like her brownies."

"I know you do. I'm glad you weren't hurt badly. Were you brave at the doctor's?"

"Yes, and I gots to ride in a amb'lance with the siren on. Aunt Jenny was asleep, but I heard it. I thought you would come."

"I'm on my way, Angie. I have been since I spoke with you this morning. It takes a long time to get to Maine from L.A."

"Next time don't go so far away."

Out of the mouths of babes, he thought. "Yeah, next time I won't be so far away. I should get there around supper time, but I'm going to the hospital first to see Jenny."

"But then you will come here?"

"Yes, Angie, then I'll be there to see you. Let me talk to Libby again."

After filling her in with his plans and getting directions to the hospital, Connor hung up. There was nothing left to do but exist through the endless minutes until he landed in Maine.

"Jenny?"

She thought she heard Connor's voice and smiled. She'd been hoping all day she'd get to a phone to call him, but here it was hours after the accident and she didn't have the energy to pick up the receiver and dial, even if she knew the number. In the confusion earlier, she'd lost her cell phone.

Libby had told her Connor had been informed. She hoped he wasn't worried.

"Jenny, are you awake?"

She opened her eyes and looked toward the door. He stood there, dressed in black.

"Connor? What are you doing here?" It was him, not a figment of her imagination.

He crossed the short distance quickly and took in the bandage on her head, the tubes and drips ubiquitous to hospital rooms.

"I came as soon as I heard, of course. How are you?"

"Aside from a headache that won't quit, I'm fine. They say I have a concussion, so they want to watch me. That's why the headache. But the other car didn't get my leg this time."

He reached out and took her hand, holding it tightly. "I never want to get a call like that again."

"I told Libby not to worry you." Jenny gripped his hand, amazed at how much better she felt just seeing him, touching him.

"Angie called from the site before the sheriff even got there. Scared me to death."

"How is she? Libby said she's fine, but

I don't want her to fret about this. With the loss of her parents, I'm worried this will have some traumatic impact."

"She sounded fine on the phone. I'm going to the Inn when I leave here. It's not her I'm worried about."

"You came here first?"

"Where else would I go? I got here as fast as I could. L.A. is too far away."

"I've thought so these last few weeks," she said softly, taking in his worried look. "Are you all right? You look terrible."

"Thanks. I didn't stop to shave, or eat, come to that. I got the first plane out and then chartered one from Boston. Every mile of the way I worried about you." He covered their linked hands with his other hand, holding on firmly. "How are you really?"

"I'll be okay. At least you're not ranting and raving," she said with a sad smile.

"I'm sure I have no need to be. You're an adult, I assume you had a reason for being in the car. It's not like you were driving recklessly."

"Of course not, silly. I was taking Angie to school. The other car slid on the ice. Fortunately it wasn't going too fast." She shivered despite the warmth in the room.

For a second that morning, she'd relived the awful crash she and Cassie had experienced.

"The deputy in the sheriff's office thought they were," Connor countered.

"Well, maybe a little fast for the conditions, but not if the roads had been dry. They were just kids. Shaken up but not hurt."

He touched her cheek lightly. "I'm sorry you were the one hurt."

She squeezed his hand. "Thank you for coming Connor, I've missed you so much these last weeks."

"Remember our conversation about a good husband?" he asked.

She nodded.

"Well, maybe you should write an instruction book, starting with, stay in Maine."

Before Jenny could ask if he planned to do just that, Dr. Rankin knocked on the door and stepped in. He had been Jenny's family physician since she was a child. In his early sixties, he looked like the kindly man he was, with white hair and thick gray eyebrows. He wore half-glasses and was carrying her chart.

"Not interrupting, I hope?" he asked. He seemed surprised to see Connor.

"Dr. Rankin, my husband, Connor Wolfe," Jenny introduced.

Connor released Jenny's hand to shake the doctor's.

"How is she?" he asked.

"Doing better than last time," the doctor said, referring to the chart. "If you don't show any other symptoms by morning, you'll be released," he told Jenny. "I just want you near medical staff in case any other complications arise. Not that I expect any, just wish to be on the safe side."

He smiled at Connor. "How are you holding up?"

"I think it took about ten years off my life. I got here as quickly as I could, but it isn't an easy trip from L.A."

"But you're here now."

"And not berating her for something that wasn't her fault," Connor said with a quick, reassuring squeeze of his hand.

"What's that?" Dr. Rankin asked.

"Like her father did last time."

Dr. Rankin looked puzzled. "I don't understand."

"When she had the other accident, her father was furious with her, worked himself up and then died right there in the hospital room.''

Dr. Rankin looked at Jenny, obviously distressed. ''Jenny, is this true?''

She nodded.

The doctor looked at Connor. ''The accident happened in Boston. I didn't take over her care until she returned to Rocky Point a few weeks later. I knew Max had died, of course, but I'd been expecting that for years.''

''What?'' Jenny said. ''What are you talking about?''

''Your father had a bad heart, Jenny. I told him to cut out smoking, ease back on the stressful lifestyle you two had, but he never paid a bit of attention. Kept saying he had to get you to the Olympics, then you'd be set for life. I was surprised he lived as long as he did.''

''My getting injured didn't cause the heart attack?'' she asked in disbelief.

''I can't think how. He'd had several smaller ones in the years proceeding his death. I prescribed medicine, but it wasn't going to keep him living forever. Have you thought all this time you caused his death?''

She nodded slowly.

"No, Jenny, your father was living on borrowed time when he died. I didn't realize what you thought, or I'd have told you earlier. You never mentioned it."

"He never said a word," she said. "How could he be so sick and never tell me?"

"He didn't want you to know. As a doctor, I was bound by ethics to respect his wishes. He felt if you won the gold, you'd have enough endorsement contracts to set you up for life and wouldn't need him. He loved his little girl a great deal. Gave up a lot to give you the chance."

"Which I blew by going out that night," she said bitterly.

Connor squeezed her hand again. "No. The drunk who ran into your friend's car caused the accident. You were entitled to a night out."

She looked at him. "I didn't cause my dad's death," she said, testing the words.

He shook his head. "No, Jenny, you didn't." He looked at the doctor. "While we're here, has she told you her leg bothers her? Is there something more that can be done to alleviate the pain?"

"We can run some tests in the morning, before she's discharged. Another thing you should have told me, Jenny. I'll go order the tests now and we'll see what we discover. Maybe there's something beyond medication that will work. They've made great strides in surgery over the last few years."

When the doctor left, Connor leaned over and kissed her gently. "Get some rest. I'm heading for the Inn. I'll be back first thing in the morning to pick you up."

"Thanks for coming, Connor."

"You're my wife, of course I came. I'm sorry you were injured, and that I was so far away."

Duty called and Connor responded, Jenny thought sadly. He was an honorable man, doing what he thought was best for her and for Angie. His wife had needed him, and he had come.

When the crisis passed, would he'd remain as he'd said or was he already regretting their hasty marriage? It was one thing to make plans to take care of his niece, with all good intentions. But the reality might prove something different.

"I'm tired. I think I'll sleep," she said, releasing him. It was enough he'd come, she didn't need him to hold her hand and pretend a concern he didn't possess.

"I'll be here first thing to take you home," he said.

"No, wait until I call. If the doctor has extensive tests to do, it could take a while."

He frowned, then nodded once. "Feel better," he said.

Jenny watched him walk away, wishing she could call him back and ask him to hold her. She had had weeks to regret her impetuous revelation that last night. It obviously had spooked him enough he'd fled to the opposite coast. How long would he stay this time? Had she made a mistake in insisting Angie would be better off living in Rocky Point? Children moved all the time. They were most adaptable. Maybe Angie would love Los Angeles. Instead of skating, she could learn to surf.

It was late the next morning when Jenny was released. She'd slept through the night, except for the checks by the nursing staff. The battery of tests Dr. Rankin ordered had gone smoothly. He had stopped in to see her before releasing her and told her about one of the new techniques in laser surgery that might help her particular situation.

Connor arrived in his rental car, and soon had Jenny at the Inn. He parked right at the base of the shallow steps leading up to the double doors.

"Want me to carry you?" he asked.

"No. I'm fine, really. Even my headache's gone." She had told him that, but he seemed to find it hard to believe.

She entered the Inn. Libby hurried over to greet her, asking how she felt. Connor joined them after parking the car.

"I think she should go right up to bed," he said.

"I would like to sit down, but I do not want to go to bed," Jenny protested. "I can rest on the sofa in the sitting room for a while."

"Want a magazine or something?" Libby asked.

"No, I don't feel up to reading yet."

Connor hovered over her as she climbed the stairs and escorted her to the sitting room.

"Don't let stubborn pride keep you up," he said. "If you need to rest, go to bed."

"Don't fuss. You probably have a lot to do, having left L.A. so abruptly yesterday. Don't let me keep you. I'm fine."

He went still, a curious expression on his face. "I do have some things to take care of. If you're sure?"

Jenny nodded. She sat upright until he left, then sagged against the cushions, resting her head on the back, closing her eyes. There was no reason to feel so disappointed he'd taken her suggestion and run with it. If he'd wanted to spend time with her, he would have said to hell with work and sat down.

There were a lot of things she needed to deal with concerning the accident. She had to contact her insurance agent and get started on a settlement so she could buy a new car. She'd get another just like the one she'd had. It'd been totaled in the crash, but had protected her and Angie, not crumpled into a steel tangle like Cassie's car had in Boston.

Angie was in school. Connor had assured her she was fine, and excited to show off her stitches to her classmates. Jenny was relieved that the child had weathered the accident so calmly.

Restless, she rose and went into the bedroom. She wore clean clothes Connor had brought, but she wanted to change her shoes into something more comfortable. Looking around, she didn't see Connor's duffel bag, or any of his clothes.

She crossed to the phone and called the front desk.

"Libby, is Connor still here?"

"I haven't seen him since he went up with you. Did you check in room seven?"

"Room seven?"

"He said he'd stay there while you were convalescing. He said he had work to do that would bother you. I thought giving him that room would be okay since we aren't crowded this week."

"It is okay, I just didn't know." Slowly she hung up the phone. Had he requested a separate room because of his concern for her? Or to keep the distance he'd established by leaving so abruptly three weeks ago? Could he not even bear to stay in the same room as she?

Jenny ate a light lunch and then lay down. Her headache had returned. Maybe a nap would help. She had not seen Connor since he brought her home.

Angie woke her up when she got home from school.

"Are you okay?" she asked.

"I'm fine," Jenny said, sitting up in bed and propping herself against the headboard. "How are you?"

Angie held up her arm. "I have stitches. It doesn't even hurt anymore."

"That's good."

"I called Uncle Connor on your phone, but he didn't come for a long time."

"He was far away, it takes a long time to get here from California."

"Next time I'm calling Libby. Can you put her phone number in your phone?" Angie asked, sitting on the side of the bed as if settling in for a long conversation.

"I sure can. And we can program in Cilla's phone and Andy's."

"And the sheriff, 'cause he was the first to come help us."

"But Connor tried," Jenny said. "He came as fast as he could."

"Which wasn't fast enough," he said from the doorway.

"Hi, Uncle Connor," Angie said, smiling happily. "Auntie Jenny is fine."

"You should let her rest," Connor said.

"I'm ready to get up," Jenny protested. She hated being in bed, feeling at a distinct disadvantage.

"Angie, run along and see if Mrs. Thompson has something for you to eat. Jenny and I need to talk."

Jenny felt her heart drop. She wished she

had feigned sleep and could pull the covers over her head. If Connor felt a need to talk, it was serious. Did it mean he wanted to end their relationship? His three weeks in Los Angeles had shown him getting married had been a foolish move. His taking another room when returning to Rocky Point had given her a clue. She had just hoped she'd been reading the signs wrong. But the look on his face warned her she wouldn't like what she was going to hear.

"I'll be out in the sitting room in a minute," she said, swinging her legs over the side of the bed. She would not have this discussion in the bedroom.

He nodded once and left.

Jenny put on her shoes and went to the dresser. She brushed her hair, staring at her reflection, not seeing much of anything. She took a deep breath. No matter what, she would not cry. At least not in front of Connor. He'd given her more than she'd ever expected. It wasn't his fault he didn't love her. That he'd changed his mind about staying married. She'd thought giving him space would be the way to go. Should she have tried another tactic?

How foolish, a person could not make someone else love them.

She headed for the sitting room.

Connor stood by the window, one forearm braced against the frame, staring out over the snowy landscape.

She went to stand beside him.

"What does it look like in summer?" he asked.

"Lawn to the road. Several flower plots, and flowers all along the house. Max does a terrific job keeping up with everything. We have groups of Adirondack chairs on the lawn for guests to sit out in the evenings."

You would see, she thought, in a few short months—if you were still here. But she had a feeling Connor would never see the Inn in summer.

The silence stretched on for several minutes. Jenny began to wonder if he was going to speak at all.

Finally he turned slightly to face her. "I don't know where to begin," he said.

For the first time since she'd met him, he looked at a loss. Despite his thoughts to the contrary, Connor was kind. He knew because she loved him that his leaving would cause her pain. But better to have a clean cut than drag it out.

"Just say it and leave, for heaven's sake," she snapped.

He looked puzzled. "Say it and leave? Wouldn't you want me to stay?"

"Why? For Angie? You can leave her here."

"What are you talking about? I'm not leaving her."

"Just me." She looked out the window. Of course he'd take Angie with him, she was his niece. Jenny thought of the time they'd spent together before he'd left. They had made headway into becoming a family. Angie would do fine with Connor.

"I'm not leaving you, either."

She swung around, her eyes seeking his.

"You aren't leaving me?"

"Jenny, are you all right? Did that blow to the head addle your mind?"

"What did you have to tell me, I thought you were leaving," she said. Hope began to blossom once again.

"I'm not leaving. I've been making arrangements to move my company here. Since we didn't find suitable office space, I'm building a small office complex that will suit us. Signed the paperwork this morning before I came to pick you up."

"You're staying in Rocky Point?" she asked incredulously.

"Didn't we discuss that weeks ago? What did you think I was doing?"

"Staying in L.A."

He frowned and rubbed a hand against the back of his neck. "I know it looked that way these last few weeks. But I was winding things up. And frankly I didn't know what to do about you."

"About me?"

"You said that last night that you loved me. Was it only passion speaking?" His eyes locked with hers.

Jenny shook her head slowly, her gaze never leaving his. Her heart began to pound.

"Well, the thing is," he said slowly, reaching out to draw her closer, wrapping his arms around her and resting his forehead against hers.

"The thing is your accident scared the daylights out of me. That flight to Boston was the longest in the history of mankind. All I could think of was what if you weren't in the world with me anymore. I don't think I could stand that, Jenny."

She swallowed hard.

"I shouldn't have been in L.A. I should

have been the one driving Angie to school. You need me here and I need to be here. With you. With Angie.''

''Because?''

''Because I love you. I want to share my life with you. I want to know everything that goes on with you and have you know all about me. I want to see what kind of future we can build for ourselves. Here, in L.A., I don't care where, as long as you're there. Your declaration scared me. But the thought of losing you scared me even more. I'm sorry I ran. I won't ever run again. I love you, Jenny. Say you still love me.''

She flung her arms around him, holding on tightly as if for dear life. ''Of course I do, Connor. I love you and always will. Oh, I can't believe you love me. That wasn't part of the deal.''

''I'm good at making deals, and sometimes they turn out better than expected.'' He kissed her long and deeply.

When the kiss ended, he looked into her eyes. ''The office situation is dealt with. They'll break ground as soon as the weather gets better. If all goes well, we'll have the administration staff moved out by end of summer. Now we have to decide on our house. How about we meet with some builders tomorrow and design the perfect place for the three of us?''

''I'd like that. Ummm, but there's just one thing—we better make it the perfect place for the four of us.''

It didn't take Connor but an instant to grasp her meaning.

He swung her around, his laughter ringing through the room. ''You mean it?''

''Yes. One of the tests I had was a pregnancy test. It showed positive. I spoke with Dr. Rankin as soon as I came to in the hospital. He said the accident didn't put me at risk. So in a few months, we'll have a son or daughter to add to our family.''

''So out of grief and tragedy comes great happiness. I'll always miss my sister, regret we weren't closer. But I hope she can see how it all turned out,'' Connor said softly.

''We'll give Angie the best family we can,'' Jenny said.

''And keep some of that best part for ourselves, as well.'' He kissed her again, sealing the vow of happiness for all the years to come.

HARLEQUIN *Presents*

**The world's bestselling romance series...
The series that brings you your favorite authors,
month after month:**

Helen Bianchin...Emma Darcy
Lynne Graham...Penny Jordan
Miranda Lee...Sandra Marton
Anne Mather...Carole Mortimer
Susan Napier...Michelle Reid

and many more uniquely talented authors!

Wealthy, powerful, gorgeous men...
Women who have feelings just like your own...
The stories you love, set in exotic, glamorous locations...